SPECIAL MESSAGE TO READERS

SHELTER FROM THE STORM

Kim takes a job on Dartmoor, trying to hide from her unhappy past. Temporarily parted from her son, Roger, and among unfriendly country neighbours, Kim finds the loneliness of the moor threatening, especially when her new boss's girlfriend, Fiona, seems to recognise her. Again, Kim runs. But Neil, her employer, soon finds her. When Kim discovers that he, too, has a shadow in his past, she stays on at Badlake House, comes to terms with life, and finds happiness.

Books by Christina Green
in the Linford Romance Library:

TIDE OF UNCERTAINTY

CHRISTINA GREEN

SHELTER
FROM
THE STORM

Complete and Unabridged

LINFORD
Leicester

First published in Great Britain

First Linford Edition
published 1999

British Library CIP Data

Green, Christina
Shelter from the storm.—Large print ed.—
Linford romance library
1. Love stories
2. Large type books
I. Title
823.9'14 [F]

ISBN 0–7089–5408–1

Published by
F. A. Thorpe (Publishing) Ltd.
Anstey, Leicestershire

Set by Words & Graphics Ltd.
Anstey, Leicestershire
Printed and bound in Great Britain by
T. J. International Ltd., Padstow, Cornwall

This book is printed on acid-free paper

1

Kim Hearne opened her eyes as the train wheels ground over the points. She had been sleeping, taking short naps since leaving London, and now the journey was nearing its end.

'Stopping at Exeter in five minutes,' a male voice said over the tannoy.

Kim sat up, staring through the dusty window with growing apprehension. She had watched the grey London suburbs disappear two and a half hours ago with a sense of relief at leaving her past behind.

Now here was a landscape of grey skies and soggy fields. This would be a good hiding-place, but it was also a lonely, desolate land.

She remembered Roger's crumpled, tear-stained, little face as they were saying good-bye. 'Mummy, don't go — ' But she knew flight was the safest plan.

He would be happy and well cared for with Jess and young Dickie.

'Sure you know what you're doing, love?' Jess had asked. 'I mean, you're a town girl, always have been. You won't like it down there. I went to Dartmoor once for a week-end camping trip. Oh, it was horrible! All mist and spooks! Nothing happened. No one around . . .'

'That sounds just the place for me, Jess. Somewhere I can hide.'

They'd looked at each other and Kim could see the concern in Jess's eyes.

Impulsively, Kim had flung her arms around her friend's shoulders. 'Oh, Jess. You're such a pal. I couldn't have managed without you. And I know you'll look after Roger for me till I can send for him.'

Jess returned the hug. 'Course I will, love. Treat him like my own. He and young Dickie will be fine together. Now look, Kim, if you hate it down there just come back. We'll make another plan. After all, it's not as if they're going to be after you for ever. Fame's only a seven-day wonder, isn't it?'

Now the train was moving slowly into the big, canopied station. Kim left the compartment and went towards the nearest exit, still hearing the bitterness in her words as she answered Jess. 'Fame? You mean shame, don't you? Something I'll never be able to forget.'

The bag weighed heavily in her hand as she walked up the platform, although she seemed to have packed very little in it. 'I'll get you to send the rest of my stuff later, Jess, when I'm settled. Here's some money for Roger's keep. Go on, take it. I'm not quite broke yet.'

Jess, had taken the handful of money reluctantly. For a moment her brown eyes widened, and Kim knew what she was thinking. The old rapport had always been there, right from their school days when one of them would always cover up for the other's pranks.

Kim smiled wryly. 'Don't say it. If

only I'd sell my shameful story to the Press I'd be rich! It's a temptation, you know.'

'Not you, love.' Jess was serious again, her smile reassuring as she hugged Roger with one arm and her own small son with the other.

'You're not the type to blab about the past. And don't think I'll let them know where you've gone. Wild horses wouldn't make me tell those rotten bloodsuckers!'

'I suppose they're only doing their job . . . ' But it was hard for Kim to accept the constant surveillance and following that had been her lot for the past few weeks. How wonderful, now, to get away from it all.

Exeter station was draughty on this March day, and unwelcoming in its shabby anonymity. Kim turned up the collar of her coat and walked briskly over the bridge to the exit.

Well, here she was, safely delivered from the unwanted attentions of the Press who had pestered her unmercifully

4

mocking smile. 'Thought you must be. You look such a townie among us country bumpkins. I'm Mary Carew. Neil asked me to meet you. My jalopy's over there.'

'Neil?' Kim was uncertain and hung back as the older woman turned away. Was this a trick to get her alone to try and dig the sordid details of the case from her?

'Neil Leston. The man you're going to work for,' the woman said impatiently. 'Look, can we get a move on? I had to leave the stables unmanned, and I really must get back — '

'I'm sorry. Mr Leston — yes, of course.'

Kim felt a fool as she followed Mary Carew along the pavement to an elderly mud-splashed Land-Rover. Why on earth had she come?

This Carew woman was bossy and patronising, and maybe Neil Leston would be the same. Maybe Mary was Mr Leston's girlfriend — so perhaps she would be working for both of them. She didn't fancy the idea. She and Mary Carew would never get on.

A wave of home-sickness washed over Kim. She wanted to be back in London, with Roger. Laughing with Jess, back in the past, before all the horror had begun.

The pain was too much, and numbly Kim climbed into the Land-Rover, forcing herself to make conversation. 'Is it far to Dartmoor? I don't know this part of England at all.'

The windscreen wipers buzzed and a film of grime was swept away as Mary Carew drove expertly out of the station and into the stretching countryside. 'Twenty miles to Badlake House. It'll take about half an hour. Give you a chance to look at the view — if only this damned mist would lift.'

They sat in silence for a while as they sped on. Small, isolated villages flashed past, linked by a patchwork of hedged fields. Humpy hills stretched upwards towards half-concealed heights, where a wilderness unfolded below the drifts of filmy mist.

'Think you'll like it here? Not too lonely for a town girl?'

Kim heard lazy contempt in the remark and said nothing for a moment. Yes, she must look so obviously a town girl, in her high-heeled boots and trendy, casual clothes. Even her hair gave her away — shoulder-length, wavy hair, usually brushed into the latest street fashion, now limp and flat because of the mist and the wind.

If she stayed here, working for Mr Leston, she supposed she might end up looking earthy and shabby, like Mary Carew, with her green wellies and scuffed brown anorak. And that frightful headscarf.

Just for a second she was back with Jess, sharing the joke. She laughed softly to herself, then suddenly remembered where she was. But Mary Carew had heard, and was looking at her with a hard, blue gaze.

'Oh, yes, I suppose I seem a real

country bumpkin to you. Well, my dear, once you've seen what Dartmoor's like, you may have second thoughts about staying at Badlake. You need to be strong and determined to live on the Moor. It's not a place for city people. Or weaklings.'

Kim returned the stare without flinching.

'I'm sure you're right. Well, I'll just have to see how I get on — and whether Mr Leston thinks I'm suitable.'

Mary Carew sniffed, and returned her eyes to the rainswept road. 'I don't imagine you'll see much of him. He only comes down for the occasional weekend. You'll be very much on your own. Hardly the sort of job that would suit you, I wouldn't have thought.'

★ ★ ★

The Land-Rover bumped across a cattle grid and began climbing again, the misty land falling away steeply on either side of the narrow, winding road.

Kim saw a grey huddle of movement in front of the vehicle and then the brakes squealed.

'Damned sheep,' Mary Carew said. Kim stared at the bedraggled group of animals that slowly wandered across the road. Black faces, heavy fleeces, and huge blotches of colour on the rumps.

'Are they wild?' she asked curiously.

Mary Carew looked at her with contempt. 'Course not. Local stock grazing on the Moor. Just remember, when you drive here — the roads are unfenced. You've got to keep your eyes open.'

Farther on a skein of soaked ponies looked up from the verge, adding to the air of loneliness that hung in the floating mist. Kim was thankful when the Land-Rover turned off through huge, open gates, up a meandering drive, and finally halted before a large house.

'This is it. Badlake House. Thought I'd show it to you before we go on to the cottage. Neil keeps a lot of his antiques here, so the place is well wired against theft. And he has a caretaker. I expect you know that.'

The Land-Rover moved off again as Kim turned, trying to take in the vastness of the old building and wondering if she would ever grow to like the place, for at first sight it looked cold and unwelcoming.

'Caretaker?' she said quickly.

'Of course. Couldn't leave a house jam-packed with valuables without someone keeping an eye on it, could you? He's called Jake McKenzie. A rough sort of chap. And his dog's the same, really wild. But at least he keeps intruders at bay and doesn't bother anyone.'

Now they were driving through neglected parkland. Immense trees of many varieties loomed through the mist. Kim thought about this new development. 'He lives there? In the house?' she inquired.

'Has the basement flat.' Mary smiled

wryly. 'Don't worry, he's not likely to bother you. A woman-hater, so I'm told. And he's lame. And as your cottage is a good quarter of a mile from the house he's not likely to try to molest you in your bed . . . '

Around the next bend a small lodge came into view. 'Here we are — Badlake Lodge.' Mary braked outside the cottage and got out briskly, clearly impatient to get back to the stables she'd mentioned earlier. 'I've got the key . . . '

Kim followed her to the door. Mary stuck her head inside. 'Smells a bit musty. Ages since the last tenant moved out. Once you get a fire going it'll be O.K. Well, I'll be on my way. 'Bye.'

Kim picked up her bag and stepped into the hallway. She turned to say goodbye, but Mary Carew had already gone and now she was alone.

Reluctantly, Kim shut the paint-flaked door and went further into the shadowy cottage. Inside, she stared at the stone fireplace, roughly laid, with a couple of giant logs on the hearth, at the little window with faded chintz curtains once blooming with scarlet roses now reduced to a sombre grey-pink muddle of shapes, and then to the two sagging armchairs standing each side of the fireplace.

A spirit lamp with a large, smoke-stained glass funnel dominated the round table on the far side of the room, and a black, hairy rug was the only concession to carpeting on the worn, wooden floorboards.

And then she noticed the silence. It was terrifying for a girl brought up in the bustle of a city. No sound at all, just the murmur of the weather outside, a drip somewhere upstairs, and the occasional creak, as if the cottage's old timbers were complaining in their sleep.

She walked to the window and looked out over the grey, deserted parkland. Would she ever get used to this?

Suddenly she caught her breath. Out of an overgrown mass of greenery, a large

16

brown dog appeared, its ears pricked and hackles up, obviously poised for action. As Kim watched, fascinated, the dog looked towards the cottage and growled as it met her gaze.

Then, as suddenly as it had appeared, it turned and vanished. Kim shivered. That must be Jake McKenzie's wild dog.

Kim's heart sank. Had she done the right thing? It would be so easy to take the next train back to town, stay with Jess again and make another plan. At least she and Roger would be together.

She went into the small, lean-to kitchen that opened out of the front room and then came to an abrupt stop. The wooden draining board of the old, stone sink was piled high with groceries.

Tea, a brown teapot, a pint of milk, and the last word in electric kettles — and against the teapot stood an envelope addressed to Miss Wilding.

Kim's cold fingers fumbled as she opened it. Then, as she read the neatly written words, she began to relax, and a tentative smile lit up her face. Perhaps things weren't quite as bad as she had thought.

Dear Miss Wilding,
Welcome to Badlake Lodge. Please make yourself as comfortable as you can and, when you are ready, go up to the House. There's a car which you can use as required.

The village is a mile down the road, turning left outside the gates, and I have an account at the general shop. I shall be coming down this week-end and look forward to seeing you. Perhaps you would be kind enough to prepare . . .

There followed a small list of duties, and the letter ended with the friendly words, *Don't let Dartmoor's changeable weather put you off before you get to know it properly! It can be very beautiful here.*
Sincerely,
Neil Leston.

Half an hour later Kim sat by the crackling log fire drinking tea and giving rein to her churning, restless thoughts. The fact that she had the use of a car cheered her a little. If she decided to leave it could take her back to Exeter station. Or if she decided to stay it would give her access to the village — and to people.

Kim frowned, refilling her mug. Could she stay in this end-of-the-world, damp, and fearsome place? At least no one could find her here.

Later, reinforced by the tea and the gentle warmth of the fire, she decided to go to Badlake House and see what it was like. Although her first impression had been that it was dark and gloomy, perhaps she would feel more friendly towards it once she was inside, as indeed she already did about the cottage.

The shadows were lengthening in the drive, as she locked the front door behind her and headed for the house. It would be tea-time back in

London, she thought. She pictured Roger and Dickie sitting on Jess's old couch, wide-eyed as they watched their children's T.V. programmes.

Maybe she could eventually bring Roger down here. Mr Leston sounded friendly, perhaps he wouldn't object to a child who was well-behaved and quiet. She and Roger together again —

By the time Kim reached the front door of Badlake House, she felt light-hearted. Reaching out a hand to lift the ornately-wreathed black knocker she paused. She had a feeling that she was being watched and she turned, staring around at the dark shapes of trees and bushes behind her with dismayed eyes.

A subdued growl made her heart beat faster. Then a man's low voice came out of the darkness and she shrunk back towards the door.

'Get back, Brutus!' There was a long, terrifying pause.

'Miss Wilding?' a voice said.

Kim stood rooted to the spot. How did this stranger know her name?

'Miss Wilding?' Again it came, louder this time, more insistent.

Kim fought the dryness in her mouth.

'Y — Yes. I'm Kim Wilding. Who are you?' A figure stepped out of the shadowy darkness and stood looking at her, the dog a dim shape at its side.

'Jake McKenzie, Mr Leston's caretaker. Thought you'd be coming around, so I've got the key. I'm a bit lame, Miss, so excuse me not walking down to the cottage to welcome you.'

She wanted to laugh, so great was her relief. So this was the wild, woman-hating McKenzie. He sounded gentle and friendly, even though his deep voice had the rough accent of a countryman. Kim ran down the steps to meet him.

'Oh, Mr McKenzie, I'm so glad to meet you! I'm not used to the country, and this mist is so deceptive — You startled me at first . . . '

A wet nose touched her hand and made her jump. 'Will it bite? It looks very fierce — '

Jake McKenzie pulled at the dog's lead and immediately it sat down, amber eyes watching Kim's every move, but obedient and seemingly docile.

'Brutus does what I tell him, Miss. But remember, he's a Doberman, a trained guard dog, so don't take no liberties with him.'

'Don't worry, I won't!'

'Excuse me, Miss.' The man limped up the steps and passed Kim, opening the door and going forward to switch on the light of the vast hall that stretched before her.

'If you'll just wipe the mud off your shoes, Miss — '

Kim did as she was told, taking the opportunity to look at her companion as she did so. Jake McKenzie was stocky and unremarkable, save for his grizzled, dark beard and long hair.

She put him down as in his mid-forties, unconventional but harmless. And yet Mary Carew had said he was a rough sort. There was some mystery here, Kim sensed.

As he led her from room to room, explaining the layout of the house as he did so, she found herself filled with a sense of wonder and admiration,

Badlake House was beautifully and elegantly furnished with antiques of all sorts. Chinoiserie gleamed in the big drawing-room, blue and white vases and dishes set off to perfection by the subdued polish of eighteenth-century furniture.

In the morning-room, farther down the wide passage, exquisite French porcelain changed the atmosphere to one of more civilised elegance, with glowing pictures complementing the evocation of a past age.

Jake McKenzie paused to unlock another room — at the end of the passage. 'Mr Leston's study,' he said and stood back as Kim entered.

Her eyes widened. Here was yet another step into the past. Victoriana of all kinds filled the room, causing Kim to wonder what sort of man Neil Leston must be. She merely glanced at the ornate fireplace, decorated with flowers and swathes of foliage, at the buttoned velvet chairs, full of over-blown fat cushions and shawls. Even the curtain hangings of rich crimson chenille with gilt tassels and thick walnut pole fittings failed to impress her.

Her whole attention was immediately caught by the pale faces that stared back at her from portraits on the patterned walls and faded sepia photographs above the fireplace and on every available inch of space. Desk, mantelshelf, occasional tables and whatnot, were all covered with photographs.

Kim went from group to group very slowly, looking intently at the Victorian faces that gravely stared back at her. A child with such vitality that she felt it might easily bounce out of its silver frame; a long-faced woman, elegant and sad-eyed; a man with blond moustache and sideburns, resplendent in tall collar. They all watched her as she inspected them, finally turning to Jake with a curious smile.

and glanced his way.

As she had expected, an expression of scorn settled on his face. She drove off without a backward look in his direction. Damn the man — she could manage her job without him, thanks very much.

The village shop was small and packed with a variety of goods that fascinated Kim as she entered. It smelled of home-cooked ham and paraffin, of oranges and mothballs. Presiding over the Post Office counter, an elderly woman watched Kim intently.

'Mornin'.' The soft, country-burred voice was wary and suspicious, and Kim held her head a little higher.

'Good morning. I'm Kim Wilding, from Badlake House. Mr Leston has asked me to do some shopping for him.'

She saw the suspicion replaced by open curiosity. 'Oh, yes, we heard you'd come. Got a list, have you?'

How had the woman heard, Kim thought as she watched the order being organised and packed into a box.

A pretty girl, dressed in riding breeches and wearing a hard hat breezed in. 'Hi, Gladys! Just off to the stables — keep me a brown loaf will you, love? Thanks. Oh, and I hear Neil's new girl has arrived safely.

'Jake was at the pub last night, said he doesn't see her staying. Too townie. Oh, golly, have I said something? I mean — gosh! Sorry, I didn't know. Well, I'd better be off. 'Bye, Gladys — '

Kim's amused eyes met those of the woman who was putting the last item into the box. 'Sounds as if I'm written off already,' she said wryly. 'Haven't really given me a chance, have they?'

Gladys tucked the bill among the groceries and allowed a small, tight smile to lift her thin lips. 'Dartmoor folks is always suspicious of townsfolk,' she said. 'You'll get used to it. If you stay.'

Kim drove back to Badlake House feeling the old anxiety growing inside

30

her. They didn't like her. Didn't expect her to make the grade. And perhaps they were right . . . it was so quiet here, so terribly open and empty.

She parked the car and carried the box towards the back door to which Jake McKenzie had given her a duplicate key. A wind had risen, shaking the bare trees and rattling the long, grey branches against each other.

The eerie silence was becoming unbearable. She longed for a radio, to hear the familiar, jokey DJ and brash, noisy music which had always filled her days at home. She couldn't stay here alone. She'd go mad! She needed people, noise, activity.

The kitchen was warm and unexpectedly welcoming. She made coffee and sat in a creaking cane chair, wondering bleakly about her future.

Were the reporters still crowding around Jess's little semi in Hampstead? Had they followed Roger and Dickie to school, asking stupid questions?

31

'Tell us about your dad.'

'Where's your mum gone, then, eh? Going to see her soon, are you? On the train? Bus? On the plane, perhaps, eh?'

She shut her eyes as the old horror returned. Had she been right to leave Roger there, with Jess and Dickie? Was he missing her as badly as she missed him? But at least he was settled at school, he had Dickie for company, and Jess was as good a mother-figure as anyone could be.

If only she could make up her mind what to do. But during the past terrible weeks, she'd had to make decisions quickly. She lived day to day, reacting to situations as they arose. Like taking this job.

The door latch rattled and Jake came in, Brutus equally silent at his side. He stood there, looking down at Kim with expressionless eyes. 'So you got back safely.'

Irritated, she snapped back quickly, 'Surprised? I suppose you expected me to get lost. Well, I'm here, and I've got all the groceries.'

If he resented her sharpness, he didn't show it. 'Mr Leston phoned. They'll be here after lunch. Put the car away if you're not using it, will you? He doesn't like to see things untidy.'

Kim watched the shaggy figure turn and leave the room.

They? Did that mean Mr Leston had a wife? But the house was so strictly masculine. Kim got to her feet and set about completing the tasks she had still to do.

Halfway through the morning she braved the empty silence of the great outdoors and went into the drive to pick the first of the pale-pink camellias that covered a huge, green shrub with buds. That was what Badlake House needed, she thought quickly — a woman's touch. Flowers, to soften the perfection of the solid, hard furniture.

Her bunch of masterkeys gave her access to the study as well as the other rooms. Kim placed the beautiful flowers, in a small vase, among the photographs on the table beneath the window and paused to admire the effect before locking up and returning to the kitchen for her lunch.

★ ★ ★

At 2.40 exactly a shiny black Porsche pulled up outside the front door and Kim stood nervously in the hall as Neil Leston breezed in.

He wasn't at all what she expected. A dark, enigmatic-looking man in his late thirties, he looked more like a city whizzkid than the retired, professional man she had imagined. And he wasn't alone. Following closely behind him appeared a stylish woman, dressed in designer clothes, the halo of soft, bubbling blonde hair setting off her beautiful, flawless face.

Neil Leston paused for only a moment then walked towards Kim, holding out his hand and smiling with what she sensed was a natural friendliness.

'Miss Wilding. Glad to meet you. I've been wondering how you're getting on. Fiona, darling, this is Kim Wilding. I told you about her. Miss Wilding, this is my fiancée, Fiona Cartwright.'

'Hi.' Kim refused to allow the opulent Fiona to sap her already depleted confidence. But she saw a calculating look flit over the lovely face.

'Have you settled in at the cottage? A pity the weather was so unwelcoming,' Neil Leston continued.

'Yes, thanks. And it's fine today. Of course, I haven't seen much of the Moor yet.'

'So you're intending to stay? Neil darling, you've found your mother's help at last!' There was such mockery in Fiona Cartwright's light voice that Kim blinked and stared as the girl shrugged out of her long, loose tweed coat and headed for the drawing-room.

'We'd like some coffee, Miss Wilding,' she said airily. 'If it's not too much trouble . . . ' Her voice wafted back and Kim noticed that Neil Leston looked uncomfortable.

'It's been a long drive,' he said quietly.

Despite her uneasiness, Kim warmed to him. 'Of course. I'll get it at once.'

When she carried the tray back to the drawing-room, Fiona was standing in the big bay window.

'You know, Miss Wilding, you remind me of someone,' she said carelessly, and wandered over to where Neil Leston sat, glancing at the morning's paper. 'Are you a model doing a spot of slumming? An out of work actress?'

Her eyes met Kim's and she smiled unpleasantly. She put a hand on Neil's shoulder. 'Perhaps a baddie on the run?'

The tinkling laugh which accompanied the words only jarred Kim the more. She slopped the coffee as she poured it, and banged down the pot on the brass tray.

Helplessly, she looked first at Fiona's wondering face, and then down at Neil. He was staring up with a frown, but whether his displeasure was occasioned by Fiona's tasteless remarks or by Kim's mismanagement of the coffee, she was never to know.

Suddenly, all her haunting fears came to a head. She couldn't stay here a minute longer. They knew, they knew!

Kim ran out of the room, not knowing what to do or where to go. She only knew she must get away. Outside, the sun gleamed fitfully on the windscreen of the Capri.

Never mind the few clothes and belongings left at the cottage — nothing mattered save her freedom, and the urgent need to escape the dawning recognition that had been in Fiona Cartwright's hard eyes.

She drove fast and uncaringly. Luckily no livestock wandered over the winding moorland roads as she swept past, her heart beating, her mind refusing to think clearly.

She would find a signpost and head for Exeter. A train back to London — and to Roger.

But the moorland roads were difficult and unmarked. Ten minutes after leaving Badlake House behind her, Kim realised she was being followed. She stared, agonised, into the mirror and saw a sleek, black car driving relentlessly on her tail. It was a Porsche and there was a man at the wheel.

Neil Leston was following her. She had no idea where she was or where she was going. Was it always to be like this, running away from her past and the shame of what she had done?

2

Kim was so distressed that she lost all sense of direction and, with a feeling of near-panic, soon found she had left the road and was driving along a bumpy track which grew worse with every passing minute. Finally the car stalled and ground to a halt on bleak, bare turf that stretched endlessly whichever way she looked.

In the far distance, a shaft of sunlight gleamed on the rocky crown of an immense, shadowy hill, emphasising the solitude of the landscape. Some ponies, black, brown, and grey, wended their way through foxy-brown dead bracken, and from afar came the sound of water, rushing down from the hidden heights of the Moor.

Kim sprang from the Capri and, as she did so, heard a car draw up. Wild-eyed, she turned round. Neil Leston was bringing the black Porsche to a halt just behind her. Oh, God, she couldn't face him yet! She turned again, ready to run into the silent wilderness, but his voice stopped her.

'Don't go any farther. It's boggy and very dangerous.' Then he was at her side, looking down with a slight smile that made her feel uneasy. Surely he was going to say he knew who she was? But, no, instead his dark eyes only looked concerned. 'Look, Miss Wilding, I know Fiona's a bit outrageous at times, but surely you're over-reacting?'

Dazed, Kim didn't know what to say. She had expected accusations not excuses. 'Oh, yes — of course,' she muttered. She realised now that she had nothing to fear from this pleasant, quietly-spoken man, who looked at her with obvious sympathy and friendliness.

He ran a hand through his black hair. 'The truth is, Miss Wilding, that I badly need someone at the house to cope with visiting clients in my absence and you seemed to be fitting the bill so well. You sounded right when we first spoke over the phone and this week-end is proving that I was right.

'So I do hope you'll agree to overlook Fiona's stupid remarks? It's difficult these days to find someone of integrity, someone completely trustworthy.'

He held her gaze and Kim had to suppress a delighted gasp. Integrity, he'd said. She smiled with relief. 'Well, thank you. If that's how you feel, of course it makes a difference. I mean, I didn't expect to — to — '

And then suddenly she was weeping, the emotional toll of the past weeks at last catching up with her. All her defences collapsed and she was unable to stop the flow of tears.

It was so long since anyone had shown anything but contempt or pity for her. Her lawyer, the police who had interrogated her at such length, and even the judge himself — although he directed the jury to bring in a verdict of manslaughter and not murder — had shown no real concern for her. Now, in her confusion, she tried to explain to this kindly stranger just why she was behaving so strangely.

'I need to — to start again, you see. And your job seemed right. But, oh it's so quiet here, so lonely, and I miss Roger so much. Then your fiancée said . . . ' The tears stopped but sobs still wracked her. 'She said my face was familiar, and so I thought that she, or you — '

This was the fearful moment when she must tell the truth and reveal her true identity. 'You see, I'm the girl who — '

'Look, I don't care a damn about your private life,' Neil Leston interrupted. He reached out to pull her against him. 'Cry if you want to. You'll feel better if you let it all out. Go on. Don't mind me.'

Kim lay weakly against his chest, hearing the steady beat of his heart beneath the pale-blue cashmere sweater.

Just for a moment she forgot who she was, who Neil Leston was. They were simply a man and a woman, thrown together by Fate. It seemed so comforting that he should be here when she so badly needed strength and reassurance. And he was right. Once all her tears were spent, she began to feel better.

Strong enough to allow forbidden memories to come surging back. Strong enough, to remember when last she had been close enough to a man to hear his heartbeat, and to feel his breath on her cheek, the comfort of a hand on her own chilled and trembling body.

Bruce, she thought, oh, Bruce, once you and I were like this . . .

★ ★ ★

She had known Bruce Hearne all her life from the time when, at her first Christmas party, he burst her balloon with a pin and then, seeing her distress, apologised at once.

'Sorry. Here, you can have mine if you like — '

His was a shrivelled green sausage, hers had been beautifully round and orange, like the sun on a summer's day, but, even at five years old, she had fallen instantly for his charm.

'Th — thank you. My name's Kim,' she hiccuped.

'Mine's Bruce. D'you want some more of that jelly?'

And so their friendship had begun, developing through the years into deep love.

'You've got to marry me, Kim. I can't manage without you.'

At nineteen and a half, Bruce was handsome beyond words, his tall and athletic physique shaped by the boxing which was his one passion in life. He trained every evening, expecting Kim to be waiting when he'd finished, pulling her close to him in a joyous celebration of their togetherness.

'I'm not going to marry you while you're dashing all around the country like this — Leeds last week, Cardiff next weekend . . .'

Even as she said these words she knew she would give in. His boxing was everything to him and she couldn't stand in his way. It wasn't their first argument, nor their last, but, as usual, she lost it.

'I can't help being away, love. Boxing's something I've got to do. The fight business is in my blood. Both the old man and his brother were heavyweights. Well, you've seen the photos and cups. I've got to get out there and win, Kim . . .'

Bruce had stared deep into her eyes. 'I'm going to be a champion,' he had said quietly. 'Nothing's going to stop me.'

Kim had nodded slowly, accepting the inevitable. She knew him so well, knew his ambition was strong enough to carry him to the top. His trainer shared the same belief. Well, she wouldn't be the one to stop him, for she loved him, just as he said he loved her.

The one thing that worried her in those early days was Bruce's reactions on the rare, bad days when he didn't win . . .

'All in the game,' Stan Pearce, his trainer always said, but Bruce took his defeats hard. He sulked, drank too much and took his moods out on Kim.

But at the beginning of their marriage, when everything was going well, when they were young and so much in love, the world was a place of light and beauty. Only later did the shadows appear, and lengthen.

It had been just like this, Kim remembered now, unaware of the smile touching her lips, when Bruce held her. The same warmth, the wonderful, shared feeling and understanding. Oh, God, if only she could go back to it . . .

Opening her eyes, she stared at Neil Leston's lean, elegantly boned face, and flushed a deep crimson.

'I'm sorry! I didn't think — '

Pulling away, she turned towards the empty landscape, blushing furiously. What must he think of her, nestling in his arms, imagining he was Bruce?

Once more she forced herself to look at him and apologise, but the confused words died on her lips as she saw the expression in his eyes and realised that he understood. His calm voice brought a measure of relief to her guilt and bewilderment.

'You don't have to explain. I've been through the mill myself. I know how it is when you reach the end of your endurance. I'm just glad I was here when you needed someone.'

A moment later he stepped back as if to distance himself from her, to maintain once again the working relationship.

'Now, I'd like an answer about the job,' he said crisply. 'You'll appreciate that I'm a busy man. I have premises in town where I hold sales, but many clients — and particularly those from abroad — prefer to come down to

47

Badlake and see the antiques in a more peaceful setting. And I don't care to visit the house too often myself.'

Kim was sure she heard a note of bleakness in the last few words. Was it possible that such a prosperous businessman could have some sort of chip on his shoulder, too? Were they alike in having pasts they wanted to forget?

She watched how he avoided her eyes as he turned back to the parked cars, so that she had no choice but to go with him.

'So, yes or no, please. I'd like you to decide now, while we're here, on our own . . .'

He turned to her, his dark eyes stern now, and for a second Kim wondered if she had only imagined the kindness he had shown so recently. But then he gave her a warm smile as he added wryly, 'How can I persuade you?

'Look — if it's the loneliness of the place that bothers you, why don't you invite a friend down to stay for a week or two? At my expense. You see, I'm so sure you're the right person for the job . . . '

Kim felt her spirits rise. A friend? Why, she could have Roger down for the half-term holiday at Easter! And then, perhaps, she could persuade Neil Leston to let him stay.

There was a school not far away. She'd seen the children in the bus one morning. Oh, to have Roger with her. They could explore this strange new world together.

She beamed at him. 'Thank you. That's most considerate of you. And I don't mind the loneliness. It's just what I need at the moment. Yes, I'd like to take the job.'

She longed to explain her behaviour and make him realise just how much she appreciated this chance to start anew, but Neil Leston had swung open the door of the Porsche and turned away, so that his voice was only just audible.

'You're not the only person in the

49

world with an unhappy past.'

Over his shoulder, he fixed her with a bleak stare. 'You're lonely?' he asked quietly. 'Well, you may find it better to be alone with nature than constantly rubbing shoulders with unwanted friends and family.' His eyes took in the sweeping landscape. 'In time you may find the Moor comforting rather than frightening.'

Together they stood in silence, while his words echoed in the cold air. Then he breathed in the fresh, sharp air and Kim knew he was again the businessman, impatient to return to his chosen, closeted life.

'Well, Miss Wilding, let's get back to Badlake, shall we? Fiona will be wondering where on earth I am.'

They drove back in convoy, and as the Porsche led the way across the moorland roads, Kim pondered over what had just happened.

Her opinion of Neil Leston, initially that of a man of the world, had deepened. Now she realised that he was a person of many parts; modern, sophisticated, and businesslike, but also surprisingly understanding, wise, and friendly.

Also, there was the hint that he disliked his beautiful home, the study of which was crammed with family relics. She remembered his bleak remark about unwanted family and friends, and wondered all the more. And the more she thought, the more she became convinced that she and Neil Leston had a lot in common.

* * *

Kim parked the Capri in the garage at the back of the house, glad to have an excuse to go indoors alone. She felt drained after her experience out there on the moor.

Now she needed to be alone to sort out her feelings, and come to terms with the fact that for the moment, her past was still a secret. Without doubt, Neil Leston's matter-of-fact dismissal of it had somehow created a new source of strength within her.

When tea-time came, she felt refreshed and more confident. She had spent a couple of hours exploring the house, immersing herself in the atmosphere of the antique decor.

In the long, silent library she had found an informative book which soon absorbed her, and she sat by the window overlooking the garden until the chiming of a long-case clock in the corner reminded her of her duties, and she hurried to the kitchen to put on the kettle and prepare the tea tray.

She was surprised to find Jake already there, his large, square hands unexpectedly careful as they laid out the delicate, white, floral-patterned, bone-china tea service. He glanced up.

'Didn't know where you were. I'll leave it to you now, though.'

'Thanks. I forgot the time.' She saw the bushy eyebrows rise and added defensively. 'I was reading about antiques. After all, if I'm going to show clients around, I need to learn about them — and fast.'

The kettle began its soft hum as they stared cautiously at each other.

'So you're staying,' Jake said quietly.

Kim stiffened. 'Sorry if you don't approve,' she said frostily.

'I didn't say that, Miss. Actually I'm glad.'

'Oh.' Kim made the tea, thankful for the opportunity to turn away and hide her confusion. She hadn't expected woman-hater Jake McKenzie to say any such thing. She placed the ornate silver teapot back on its matching silver tray and shrugged. 'Sorry I snapped your head off. I'm a bit on edge these days.'

'I know.' A hint of a smile played about his lips.

'How d'you know?' She looked up at him challengingly.

'I know about animals,' Jake said, his eyes twinkling. 'People aren't all that different.' He turned away. 'Mind that step as you go down the hallway, Miss,' he called.

Fiona Cartwright was curled up on the long, brown leather Chesterfield at the end of the drawing-room, her skirt and matching wrap a huddle of colour against the darkly-elegant decor. She threw down a magazine and yawned as Kim brought in the tea.

'Better late than never,' she murmured, glancing at her small gold watch.

Kim bit back an angry remark. 'I didn't want to disturb your afternoon nap, Miss Cartwright . . . ' she said politely.

Placing the tray on a small, oak gate-legged table close to the sofa, she caught Fiona's dying smile and knew she had been foolish to say anything. It would have been far wiser to ignore any such jibes and taunts if she intended to stay here. Why make matters worse by creating unpleasantness between herself and Neil Leston's fiancée?

It was Neil who saved the situation, rising from his deeply-winged armchair by the fire and coming across to where

Fiona smoothed her skirt as she sat up.

'You two ought to have something in common,' he said placatingly, 'both Londoners, both new to the country. And I don't think either of you know much about antiques, do you? Darling, I'm quite aware that the past bores you stiff, almost as much as rural Devon does! And what about you, Miss Wilding?'

Kim smiled gratefully. 'I've always had a feeling for old things, but until now they've never really been part of my life. I'm afraid you'll find me ignorant at first until I can learn all I can.'

'Just the girl to advise all those wealthy, foreign clients for you, sweetie,' Fiona said lightly, before biting into a sandwich with relish.

Kim held her tongue as Neil Leston took his cup of tea towards the fireplace. She saw he was irritated by Fiona's remark, but he only smiled at her disarmingly.

'The will to learn is all-important. There are several books in the library which will help you, Miss Wilding. And you can get me on the phone if anything crops up that you can't deal with. I'm sure we'll manage between us.'

'Thank you, Mr Leston.' Kim left the room, but not before she heard Fiona's spiteful words.

'Darling Neil, what is the point of having an assistant who has to refer back to you all the time? She'll be quite hopeless, you know . . .'

It was with mixed feelings that Kim returned to the kitchen and sat down to have her own cup of tea. She was sure Neil Leston was pleased with her so far, but there was always the risk that Fiona, very much his sort of woman, and fitting so completely into his urban life style, would eventually persuade him to see things from her point of view.

She might even force him to find someone more suited to what was clearly an important and demanding position.

Kim let her tea grow cold as she thought over the situation. She knew now that she wanted to stay here and make a success of the job.

She knew it would be interesting, and already she was feeling the stimulation and attraction of it. If the environment was slightly alien to her, she would just have to get used to it. Neil Leston had said encouraging things about the moor, and Roger was coming for Easter. Her own little Roger.

Suddenly her world — recently so dark and hopeless seemed so much brighter. She refilled her cup and drank the hot tea with enjoyment, savouring it. Yes, she was sure now that she could make a fresh life for herself, here at Badlake.

* * *

Even with the new sense of determination relaxing her, it was hard going for the rest of the weekend, for Fiona seemed intent on putting obstacles in her way. Kim forced herself to remain good-humoured, and didn't once rise to the veiled barbs, but she was increasingly aware of the growing enmity between them.

And it was Fiona who had the last word. Sweeping past Kim, who stood at the front door to bid them good-bye in the cold, drizzling Monday morning she gave Kim a cool stare. 'I shouldn't settle in here too cosily, Miss Wilding,' she murmured. 'I never forget a face — and yours doesn't fit, does it?'

Kim watched the glossy, black car nose its way down the long drive, unease growing inside her. Even Neil Leston's quiet good-bye and cheery wave did nothing to dispel the old hunted feeling. Fiona's words could only mean one thing. She wouldn't rest until she had discovered Kim's true identity.

And what then? Neil Leston would

be shocked and angered to realise that Kim had used his house as a hiding place and deceived him. She would be asked to leave, and once again she would be on the run. Except this time she had nowhere to go.

Shutting the heavy front door, Kim listlessly set about her household tasks. It was well into the afternoon before she had prepared the bedrooms for Neil's and Fiona's next visit, tidied the few rooms in use, and then inspected the larder and fridge, making a shopping list to replace stocks.

Her head ached and she was cold and depressed. Her future seemed uncertain again, but one thing she was sure of — Neil Leston would have no excuse to sack her for incompetency. She would leave Badlake House in better condition than she had found it.

By tea-time all the antiques on display were newly-cleaned and shining. The camellia bud in the study was replaced by a fresh one, and a handsome arrangement of glossy, winter foliage stood in the hall, ready to welcome any caller.

Kim left the house as dusk fell. She had half-expected to see Jake McKenzie at some time during the day, but there had been neither sight nor sound of him.

She locked the door and walked briskly down the drive, congratulating herself that she was no longer dwelling on the loneliness and possible risk of the solitary walk. Her mind was more settled now.

She must learn to take each day as it came. If the future held more shocks, then she would deal with them as they arrived. For now, she was going home to the cottage to spend a quiet evening making plans for bringing Roger down here for Easter.

As she crunched over the gravel beneath the overhanging branches of rhododendron and birch, she recalled Neil Leston's comment on loneliness and was inclined to actually agree with him. She felt strong and ready for anything.

Badlake Cottage was no longer just a shabby little house but home. Kim went in and put a match to the already laid fire before going into the kitchen to prepare her evening meal. She felt curiously elated and ready for anything. As soon as she had eaten she would telephone Jess, telling her the news and making plans for Roger to come and stay. She smiled wryly to herself.

Damn that snooty Fiona woman. She can do what she likes, I don't care. Roger and I will be together again, and that's all that matters. Easter's only a few weeks off, it's not likely that she and Mr Leston will be down again before then . . .

But her soaring spirits fell the minute she heard the tension in Jess's voice. 'Oh, Kim — I've been hoping you'd ring. Roger has been going on and on about you. He misses you so badly. And something's happened.'

Kim's throat tightened. 'He's all right, isn't he?'

'Yes, but really miserable. Look, Kim, before you speak to Roger, there's something I've got to tell you. Not very good news, I'm afraid — '

'Go on, then, I'm listening.' Kim felt all her confidence die away. Roger was unhappy. Jess had bad news. And she, fool that she was, had been so sure things were looking up. 'Jess, tell me — quickly.'

'One of those rotten reporters followed the boys to the Saturday morning film show. You know it's only just up the road — I wouldn't have let them go alone, but it's so near, and I thought all the reporters had left after you disappeared.' Kim heard the guilt in her friend's voice.

'Don't blame yourself, Jess! I know how well you look after the boys. What happened?'

'It was that ratty-faced little chap, the one that offered you the money, love. Well, he started chatting to the boys, asking them questions, and young Dickie upped and said you caught a train that left Paddington at ten-something last week.

'He must have heard us talking when he was in bed. Well, I don't suppose the chap got much out of it, but I must say I was worried stiff at first.'

'On Saturday, you said?' Kim murmured thoughtfully. 'It's Monday night now. Surely the man would have been here by now, if he was coming? Oh, don't worry, Jess, no one could put two and two together and make four from what little Dickie told him . . . '

Jess sighed with relief. 'Thank goodness you see it like that! Well, love, here's your Roger. Can't keep him off the line any longer — '

And suddenly Roger was on the line. 'Mummy! When're you coming back? It's O.K. here, but I want you to come back. Dickie's broken my torch and I was sick at school on Friday . . . '

Tears welled up in Kim's eyes. 'Roger, love, tell Jess you're going to spend Easter with me, down here in Devon. Tell her I'll write and arrange it. Darling, be good. It won't be long before we're together again. Good-bye, my love . . . '

★ ★ ★

Kim left the kiosk with a smile on her lips. She no longer noticed how dark the night was and how lonely the road that took her back to the cottage. All she knew was that Roger needed her. She saw his face, that look of Bruce's about his mouth, and her own wide-spaced, hazel eyes.

His childish words echoed through her mind, and she glowed with love for him. To have him here, in the little cottage that would so soon become their new home, would be almost too much for her to bear. It was so long since happiness had filled her life.

As she walked, well wrapped up against the blustering moorland wind, she saw a gap appear in the racing clouds overhead, and a sliver of new moon hung briefly, silver-gold and beautiful, in the heavy darkness. Warm and elated, she hurried on.

But just before she arrived at the gates that lay a stone's throw from the cottage, she faltered in her brisk stride. Was that footsteps she heard?

Quietly, she slipped into the shelter of a large bush that shadowed the far gate. It could be just a casual passer-by — someone heading for the public phone box — as she herself had done. But it might also be the reporter who had interrogated Dickie and Roger. Had he discovered her hiding-place?

Concealed behind the evergreen foliage, Kim held her breath as the steps drew nearer and then, dramatically stopped.

Cautiously, she looked out from behind the thick branches, narrowing her eyes as she stared into the darkness. Something pale moved, and she knew instinctively that it was a jumper — Jake McKenzie's dirty, off-white sweater.

He was standing at the cottage door, lifting his hand to knock. Her heart plummeted as she saw him pull a folded newspaper from his pocket.

Kim could hardly believe her bad luck. She had been so worried about Fiona recognising her, or the reporter tracing her here, that she had quite forgotten the possible danger of someone local remembering her from newspaper photographs. And now Jake had discovered who she was . . .

She groaned in despair, regretting the small sound immediately.

She shrank further into the shadows not daring to take her eyes off Jake. She saw him look around, eyes raking the shapes of the gates and the shrubs, but then he turned again to the door, evidently satisfied that what he'd heard had been merely the night cry of some bird or foraging animal.

Kim held back a sigh of relief. She would wait here until Jake, finding her out, returned to his own flat. But as she continued to watch she saw the dog, Brutus, leave Jake's side.

Slowly, but inevitably, the dog approached her hiding-place. The nearer he came, the clearer she could see him. His ears were pricked, eyes gleaming through the shadows, and his lips drawn back in an ugly snarl, showing white, fierce teeth.

3

As the dog approached her hiding-place, Kim suddenly remembered the command she had heard Jake use earlier. 'Get back, Brutus!' she cried.

The big dog stopped, head on one side, and Kim held her breath. Would the dog obey her unfamiliar voice? 'Get back,' she repeated, more loudly. Relief swept over her as Brutus obediently lay down at her feet, his sharp eyes no longer fierce and menacing.

Jake hurried up to her, staring in amazement as she sagged against the concealing tree bole. 'What on earth — ' He looked as shocked as Kim felt, and she gave a sigh of relief as she came out of the shadows towards him.

'I'd been phoning — and then I heard footsteps. I was a bit worried, so I hid.'

Jake ran his fingers through his hair. 'Well, all I can say is, it's a good job you knew how to stop Brutus attacking. He's trained to scent out anything unusual. And once he's off, well . . . '

He frowned, watching Kim intently. 'Here, let's get you inside,' he said quickly. 'Cup of good strong tea, that's what you need, Miss. Got the key? Right. I'll open the door.'

It was wonderful to sink down in the chair by the dying fire and know she was safe. Kim watched as Jake put kindling on the glowing embers, and then disappeared into the kitchen to make the tea.

When he returned, the fire was burning brightly and Brutus was stretched out in front of it, looking like part of the shabby hearth rug.

'Made himself at home, I see. Likes a wood fire, does Brutus. Come here, boy.' One snap of Jake's fingers and the dog returned to the side of the table where his master stood.

Kim took her mug of tea gratefully. God, what a lucky escape she had had. Her hands were still trembling. She saw Jake watching her, and realised quickly that he was waiting for an invitation to sit down.

'Please . . . ' She nodded at the chair opposite and he gave her a brief smile as he lowered himself into it.

'Don't want to be a nuisance, Miss. I'll drink this and then we'll be off.'

Over the rim of her mug, Kim studied him. This man was kind and thoughtful and not at all what she had been led to believe. She leaned forward and smiled at him.

'Take your time, Jake. I mean, there's no hurry, is there?'

He nodded and settled back to drink the tea with plain enjoyment. Silence fell between them, undemanding and easy. Then a log moved in the fire, sending little sparks up the chimney. As Jake turned to push the log back into place, Kim saw the folded newspaper in his pocket.

In all the excitement, she'd quite forgotten the real reason for hiding from Jake. He must know who she really was. There must be something about her in the paper, and he'd come to show it to her, to force a confrontation . . .

As if suddenly remembering, Jake pulled the paper from his pocket and unfolded it.

'Nearly forgot. Something here I wanted to show you. Let's see, where is it?'

Kim was rooted to the chair. So this was it, the very thing she had dreaded ever since she came to Dartmoor. Jake, and the rest of the village, would find out who she was and what she had done.

'Thought of you straight away, I did. Hope it isn't too late.' He was holding the page for her to see, looking at her thoughtfully.

'Too late?' She took the paper from him with shaking hands.

'Well, this is last week's, see. They

might've all gone by now.'

Kim stared blankly at the page. What was he talking about? She had expected to see her photo, or at least her name, in the paper, but instead she realised that she was looking at a page of local advertisements.

'I marked it. Halfway down, on the left — ' She glanced up, met his gaze and saw that he was smiling encouragingly.

'Found it?' he asked, and then got out of his chair to come to her side. 'There you are,' he said.

Kim read the advert with blank astonishment. *Good home wanted for kittens. Two male, one female. Black, or black and tan. Ring daytime.* And then a local number.

'Oh!'

'Worth phoning maybe, to see if they've still got one. Animals are good company, you know.'

She smiled gratefully. 'Thanks, Jake. I'll ring tomorrow.' She tried to keep her tone light. 'Yes, I'd quite like a kitten. Nice and cosy, by the fire. Something to come home to . . . '

She was saying foolish, impulsive things in order to cover her confused emotions, but if he noticed, Jake merely nodded.

'That's it. All need something, don't we? Well, I'll be off. Up you get, Brutus.'

The big dog sat up obediently, looking at Jake with intelligent eyes. 'Say good night to the lady, then,' Jake said.

A wet nose touched her hand, and the docked tail wagged briefly in friendship. Kim watched them go towards the door.

'Jake,' she called after him.

He stopped and turned.

'Thanks. It was good of you to think of me. Come again, will you?'

His face softened. 'Well, thank you, Miss. I'd like to. Used to visit old Mrs Appleby quite a bit. She was the last tenant. We were good friends. I missed her when she died.'

Their eyes met, and Kim knew an understanding had been forged between them. Jake McKenzie wasn't, after all, the woman hater she'd been warned about, merely a shy man, a loner, who possibly found it difficult to let a woman enter his life.

And then she realised that he, too, was seeing her in a new light. Opening the door to let Brutus out into the night, he said gruffly. 'I'd be glad to return your hospitality, Miss. Maybe you'd like to come and see the wood carving I do in my spare time?'

'I'd love to, Jake. Thank you. And my name's Kim, by the way.'

He nodded, looking embarrassed, but pleased. 'Kim. Right, then. See you tomorrow, eh? Good night, now.'

He was gone, the door banging behind him, the cottage suddenly empty and very quiet. Kim took the tea tray into the kitchen, saw that the fire was doused for the night, and prepared to go up to her bed.

But instead of bolting the front door,

she opened it and stepped outside into the clear, night air. At first the darkness was total and frightening, but within seconds her eyes had grown accustomed to it. She saw the outline of the gate pillars, the shapeless mass of hanging foliage, and a welcome glimmer of the barely-visible, new moon.

The silence was still there, but it was no longer as terrifying as it had seemed at first. Now it was full of murmurs and night calls.

* * *

In bed, she thought back over the day's events and knew she had made a step forward in her new life.

Dartmoor was more acceptable. She and Jake were on better terms. And she didn't have to fear Brutus . . . and there was the hope of having a kitten who would purr on her lap while she and Roger sat by the fire, sharing their thoughts and their love.

The fear that she might be recognised

was gone and she could now relax. But still it was difficult to let herself look back and remember.

Sleep eluded her and images came fast and vivid in her troubled mind. Bruce. Tonight, for some reason, the picture of him in her head was clearer than usual. Bruce, in the first years of their marriage, when his career had escalated suddenly, and the ambition, always present, became powerful and oppressing.

There had been a cat, she recalled chillingly, when they lived in the North London suburb. A large, thin, tabby called Tramp, who had invited himself into their little semi and refused to leave, despite Bruce's warnings.

'If it hasn't gone by the time I'm home tonight, it goes out the door with my foot behind it. I can't stand cats,' he'd growled.

'But why, love? Poor little thing, he's harmless, fancy living wild in this weather.' Kim had held the purring creature which was clearly overjoyed to be on the warm side of the back door for once, after weeks of living in draughty sheds and garages.

'Dirty habits, cats have got. Now look, Kim, it's got to go,' Bruce had threatened, but Kim had stoutly defied him.

'I'll keep him out of your way and I'll house-train him. We can't let him live outside again, like an old tramp. Now, that's a good name, let's call him Tramp . . .'

She had stepped closer to Bruce, smiling up at him across the soft, feline body. 'Don't be a misery, darling. You'll end up by loving him, I know you will.'

For a second, anger flashed in Bruce's eyes, and then it was gone. A good-humoured grin grudgingly spread over his face and he bent down to kiss the end of Kim's nose. 'O.K, you win. I know when I'm beaten.'

They had laughed together at the mere thought of Bruce ever being beaten, and Kim watched him leave for a training session, turning to wave and smile before he disappeared down the road.

But he had been beaten, knocked down that evening by a new sparring partner who didn't realise that the up-and-coming Bruce Hearne must always be allowed to win. By the time he came home again, Bruce was in a savage mood.

He sat opposite Kim at the fireside with a tray of soup and sandwiches on his knee, reliving the unfortunate scene. 'Stupid fool! Won't last long, that one. I told Joe so, too. 'Get him out of my way,' I said. 'I need a chap who'll take my punches, not suddenly slam 'em back when we've finished' . . . '

Kim had known something was wrong. She sat mutely, hoping his bad mood would pass.

'And I thought I said get rid of that damn cat.' Suddenly Bruce was on his feet, the tray sent flying on the hearth-rug. He was kicking out at the shadowy figure of the cat which streaked into the kitchen almost before Kim realised what was happening.

'Tramp! Tramp! Oh, Bruce, how could you? Come here, puss . . . '

'Get him out.'

They were face to face in the tiny kitchen, watching the frightened cat making a rapid escape through the half-open window above the sink, and suddenly it was more than just a stray cat now, it was a threat to their life together.

'Bruce, you've got to stop being like this. I can't take it any more. Not with a baby on the way . . . ' Kim could have bitten her tongue. She hadn't meant to blurt it out like that. But now it was said.

She waited with bated breath for Bruce's reaction. Then his face softened and he was his old self again, all tender, caring, and loving, his arms warm and strong about her, his kiss resolving all her anxieties.

'Oh, Kim! Why didn't you tell me before?'

And then, before she could answer, he swung her up, carrying her back to the fireside, putting her down as if she was something delicate and precious. So gentle. So loving.

'God, I'm pleased. Now this really is something! What'll we call her, then?

'Her? But it might be a boy, darling!' Kim smiled down at him as he kneeled by her side, smoothing her hair, holding her hands, and finally laying a big, gentle hand on her stomach.

' 'Course it'll be a girl.' Jokingly he raised his hand and, forming it into a fist, lightly brushed her nose. 'It'd better be,' he said, and they'd laughed because it couldn't really matter if this already adored baby turned out to be a boy instead of a girl.

And then Roger was born . . .

★ ★ ★

The next thing Kim knew she was waking to a bright, sunny morning full of excitement at a new day.

She hadn't felt like this for ages, glad to be alive, with so many things to do. Rushing breakfast, she arrived at Badlake earlier than usual and went straight to the library to continue her studies.

Halfway through the morning a car drew up outside, and a soft-spoken elderly American appeared at the front door. 'How can I help you, Mr . . . ?' Kim asked.

He held out a hand. 'George Stevens, that's me. And you are . . . '

'Kim Wilding.' For a second her smile faltered. '*Miss* Wilding,' she added.

'Well now, Miss Wilding, Mr Leston directed me down here. I'm looking for something special to take home to the States next week. A special something that my wife'll like. What do you suggest?'

Kim thought rapidly. 'I suggest, Mr Stevens, that you wander around the house and see what there is here. I'm sure something will catch your eye.

And how about some coffee, while you're looking?'

The bright blue eyes in the weather-beaten face twinkled warmly. 'A gal after my own heart!'

When Kim returned with the coffee a little later, she found Mr Stevens in the study. Oh no, she must have forgotten to lock it — He stood, entranced, in front of the wall covered with Victorian photographs.

'This is it!' He turned to her, grinning broadly. 'These'll look real good in my ranchhouse. All those long English faces, reminding me of my forgotten ancestors. Now — how much for the set, young lady?'

Brightly, she beamed at the American and turned away, retreating from the study, the coffee tray still in her hands as she headed for the dining-room. 'Come and have your coffee, Mr Stevens, and we'll talk about them, shall we? Cream? And sugar?'

George Stevens followed her obediently, finally sinking down heavily at the long refectory table. 'Both if you please. And now, those photographs — '

Kim looked at him shrewdly. Perhaps he was the sort of man who loved his wife, and would accept another woman's suggestion of what might be pleasing to her.

'If you really want something rare and beautiful for Mrs Stevens, may I make an alternative suggestion?'

'Sure, honey.' He spooned sugar into his cup and waited.

'Well, speaking as a woman, I'd find those dreary old photos awfully dull,' Kim said lightly. 'No colour in them. No action.'

'Now, we happen to have a particularly fine set of eighteenth-century hunting prints which really are very impressive. May I show them to you? Just an idea, of course.'

'Well, I dunno . . . ' he began, but Kim was determined.

'Let me go and find them for you. Have some more coffee while I'm gone. And help yourself to a biscuit.

I mean a cookie!' She gave him a wide smile, and saw, with relief, that he was smiling back at her. She hurried to the study and phoned Neil Leston.

'Who? Oh yes. Something wrong?' He sounded a little impatient. 'Hunting prints? Yes, a good set on the library wall. Don't let them go for under . . . '

Kim whistled at the price. 'They must be very good at that price.'

'They are. And rare, too. Actually I doubt if the old boy will come up to scratch. For all his *bonhomie*, he's a close-fisted character. Tell him they've been much admired several times before, but, so far, no one's been prepared to pay the price I'm asking.'

'I'll do my best, Mr Leston.'

'Do that, Miss Wilding. I'll ring you back later today and see how you got on. Around five-thirty.' He rang off, and Kim braced herself to meet the challenge of selling the prints to the rich American.

Finally, after a good deal of haggling, the old man grudgingly gave in. 'Okay, honey, you've persuaded me! Wrap 'em up and get 'em on the boat by next week. Now, where's my money?' Kim could have hugged him with delight.

She felt elated at her sale, and the feeling stayed with her for the rest of the morning. As the afternoon closed in, she decided to give herself an hour off and see about the kitten.

Calling at Jake's flat to ask him to keep an eye open for further visitors, she was delighted to find he'd already telephoned the number in the advertisement.

He gave her a slip of paper with an address. 'One left, you're lucky. Honey Tor Stables are down a marked track on the Widecombe road. You can't miss it. Good luck.'

To Kim's surprise, the woman she saw walking across the stable yard at the end of the moorland track, was Mary Carew. Parking the car, she hesitated for a moment. She wasn't looking forward to meeting the formidable Mrs Carew again.

But Mary was beside her, peering curiously through the window. 'Well, hello. What're you doing here?'

Kim smiled politely as she opened the door. 'Come to offer a good home for your remaining kitten, Mrs Carew.'

'Ah, so it was for you. Jake didn't say — '

'Mm, he's a man who doesn't like his left hand to know what his other one is up to! I've learned that, already!'

They looked at each other warily, and Kim's confidence returned. She felt vastly different from the anxious, lonely girl whom Mary had picked up at Exeter station. Was it really only last week?

Kim looked around her. 'This must keep you busy, Mrs Carew. I don't know much about horses, but I imagine they need a lot of attention?'

'And care. All animals do.'

She picked up the warning tone in Mary Carew's voice and held the other woman's gaze. 'How right you are. And I shall need lots of expert guidance, if I take your remaining kitten.'

Mary's mouth twitched slightly. 'Come into the kitchen. Over here. Don't mind the mud, it's a working hazard. Like a cup of tea? And while I put on the kettle you can have a word with Number Three.'

★ ★ ★

Kim stopped in the middle of the untidy kitchen, looking with interest and hoping that she wasn't showing undue curiosity. What a mess!

The long scrubbed table was heaped with letters, newspapers, and the remains of a meal. Leather tack hung from innumerable hooks on walls and the back of the door, and various sodden anoraks, woolly hats, trousers, and socks were airing on the backs of all the old-fashioned chairs.

'Number Three is the last of the litter. I don't ever give them names.' Mary cleared a space on the table, put a brimming mug down, at the same time moving a green sweater to another chair.

'Once they've got names, you get too fond of them, you see. Come here, you little monster . . . '

She bent, retrieving a small bundle of black fur that was trying to climb up her trouser leg. 'What d'you think? Strong-willed, but bright. Needs a firm hand.'

'Oh! He's lovely!'

Small, vivid eyes looked up at Kim, the tiny triangular mouth open to reveal ferociously-sharp, pearly teeth ranged above and below a rough, pink tongue. Number Three gave a miaow, and Kim knew she couldn't say no.

'He's gorgeous! Yes, I'd love to have him! Roger will adore . . . '

She stopped abruptly. 'I mean, he'll be such company. And I promise I'll look after him. You must tell me about having him doctored, or whatever the word is.'

'Neutered. Yes, I'll give you all the advice you need. Drink your tea.'

Kim knew that today she had broken down some barriers with Mary Carew. Nursing the restless kitten as she had her tea, she saw that Mary, sitting opposite, was watching her closely.

She gave her a brief smile. 'I'm glad you're having him. I wouldn't let him go to just anyone. I can trust you to look after him, though.'

'Thank you.'

Mary refilled the mugs.

'Well, how are things going? I hear you've made a good impression on Jake, that the wild dog is putty in your hands, and that you fell foul of the lovely Fiona . . .'

Mary laughed aloud at Kim's obvious surprise and resentment. 'My dear, you just have to accept village gossip! Believe me, you've done extremely well. Usually when a townie comes, she's given a hard time for a year or two. But I haven't heard a word against you. Not yet, anyway!'

Kim couldn't help joining in the laughter. She was amused, and also pleased at Mary's words. *Not a word against you*. Well, at least that was a start.

'You're obviously fitting in here,' Mary said perceptively, 'and I'm glad. You were such a poor, worried scrap when I collected you last week. Now you look altogether healthier, with some colour in your cheeks. Happier, too. What were you going to say just now about — Roger, wasn't it?'

Kim looked up into Mary's kind, intelligent eyes. There didn't seem any point in lying, and she knew that Mary would offer only sympathy and advice. 'Roger, that's right. My son — '

Mary nodded, casually, then said, very matter-of-factly, 'At school, is he? Be coming down to join you in the holidays, I dare say. Number Three will be overjoyed to have a playmate.'

Kim finally relaxed, glad to have someone to talk to. 'He's staying with a friend. In London. But I'm hoping . . . ' She held her breath. Was it foolish to spill out her plans and hopes?

'That he'll be here for good?' Mary added. 'Why ever not? The school at Widecombe is excellent. And a child brought up in the country has such a wonderful background to draw upon later in life.'

She fixed Kim with her honest gaze. 'I suppose you're afraid that Neil won't want a child around the place, not being exactly the family type. Well, if ever he complains, you can always let young Roger come here for a day. I like kids, and mine are all grown up and away now.'

'That's terribly kind of you

Mary waved aside her thanks. 'Not at all! Tell me, why did you have to leave him behind?'

Kim looked away, avoiding the directly-searching eyes. 'It wasn't convenient to bring him,' she said lightly. 'And I didn't want to upset his schooling.'

There was a long silence between them, interrupted only by the kitten's purrs.

'You've run away, haven't you?' Mary said quietly. 'Come here to make a new start. A broken marriage, was it?'

She squeezed Kim's hand. 'My dear, you're not the only one in the world, you know, to want to make a new life for yourself. It happens all the time.

'Yes, really. I was divorced fourteen years ago. I have a sister who's going through it right now. And your boss — well, Neil suffered a truly traumatic experience when his mother ran off with another man.

'His father died very soon after — I honestly believe of a broken heart, if such things are possible.'

She lowered her voice. 'Do you know, Neil's never got over the ghastly childhood he had as a result of his mother's affair. Poor love, he immerses himself in his business.

'He's highly successful and, of course, he's engaged to that awful Fiona female, but I've seen him at times when he's back there, in the past, unable to shake it off. Sad, don't you think? As I said, these things happen all the time.'

Suddenly Kim knew she had to get away. She rose, still clutching the now sleeping kitten. She was uneasy about this new information. She wanted to be alone, to think things over.

Mary produced a cardboard cat box and carried it out to the car, with Number Three now squealing loudly at having been wakened and imprisoned.

Kim turned at the car door. 'I'm terribly sorry! We haven't discussed your charge for the kitten . . . '

'Good Heavens, what an idea! I don't want anything. Just glad to get him from under my feet — '

She smiled gratefully at Mary. 'I'll ring you, if I may, when I need advice.'

Mary nodded. 'Do. If you've had a kitten before you'll know about house-training and litter trays and frequent small meals — '

'Yes. We took in a stray, once.'

Momentarily she was back with

Tramp, and Bruce's fierce temper. But some of the hurt had now gone from the memory and so, waving to Mary, and smiling down at the cardboard box on the seat beside her, Kim drove back to Badlake with her thoughts busily occupied.

She discovered that talking to Mary, even briefly, about Roger, had helped to lessen the pain of their separation. It seemed that she had made a new friend, and their recent conversation rang in her ears as she drove through the bleak, windswept landscape.

★ ★ ★

Back in the house, she headed for the study to wait for Neil Leston's call. Mary's uninhibited revelation about Neil still echoed, and Kim thought hard about the disturbed childhood he had endured. It could account for many things — his rather impersonal attitude, as if he felt the need to distance himself from people.

In case they hurt him again. Well, she knew how he felt. The ringing of the telephone broke into Kim's thoughts and she picked up the receiver, hearing Neil Leston's cool voice at the other end.

'Hello. How did you get on with the hunting prints?' She told him what had happened. 'Splendid! So our friend from the States paid up. You must tell me the secret of your sales technique!'

'I just pointed out how rare and beautiful they were, and how he'd be the envy of all his friends,' Kim said, laughing. 'Oh, and I gave him coffee and cookies . . . '

'That was what did it, of course.'

There was a long pause, then he spoke again, his voice now formal and businesslike.

'There's something I've got to talk to you about. I'll be down mid-afternoon on Friday. And I'll be alone. Is that all right with you?'

'Of course,' Kim faltered.

'Right,' he said crisply. 'Until Friday

then. Good-bye, Mrs Hearne.'

She replaced the receiver and sat there, very still, in the shadowy room. The afternoon light had gone and already night was peering through the uncurtained windows. Outside, the sound of swaying trees added to the mystery of the study.

Why should Neil Leston want to come down especially to talk to her? And without his fiancée? What on earth could he want to talk to her about?

Only then did she recall that Neil Leston had said, '*Good-bye, Mrs Hearne.*'

4

Kim sailed through the next few days, her numbed mind hardly registering all she did as she performed her duties at Badlake House and made arrangements with Jess for Roger to be put on the train on Saturday morning.

Jess sounded cheerful, and Kim, warming to her friend, was able to thank her whole-heartedly for giving her little boy a home.

'I'll always be in your debt, Jess.

'Don't be daft! You'd do the same for me. I'm going to miss him while he's away — so don't let him forget Auntie Jess and young Dickie, will you?'

'As if he would. Anyway, he's only coming for the school holiday.' Suddenly Kim decided not to tell Jess of her hope that Roger might be allowed to stay with her at Badlake permanently.

Once again, she recalled Neil Leston's curt and impersonal voice calling her Mrs Hearne and saying he wanted to discuss something with her.

If, as she feared, he was about to ask her to leave the job because of the recent court case, then Roger would yet again need Jess's hospitality and loving care.

Then Kim's worries were shattered as Roger's shrill voice yelled into her ear, 'Mum! Mum! I'm going on the train all by myself! Auntie Jess has just said — '

Kim quickly pulled herself together. 'Yes, darling, you are. She'll ask the guard to keep an eye on you and I'll be at Exeter station to meet you.' Suddenly she ached for him and her voice was choked. 'Don't talk to anyone on the train, sweetheart. Ask Auntie Jess to get a comic or something to look at. Be a good boy. I can't wait to see you!'

After ringing off, Kim sat by the fire with Number Three curled on her lap, and allowed herself to drift off into an impossible daydream. She and Roger together again, this time for good, living peacefully at Badlake Cottage free from threats from the past.

Roger would go to the village school, make new friends, and develop an interest in his surroundings. Together they would explore the vast wilderness of Dartmoor. Spring was coming, with warmth and new vitality.

The kitten stirred and, stretching, dug a sharp claw into Kim's leg, bringing her back to harsh reality. The ominous thought of what Neil Leston wanted to talk about returned, darker than ever. Dreams cast aside, she poked the dying fire and resolved not to allow herself to indulge in fantasy ever again, for she sensed that the past would not let go its hold on her so easily, or so soon.

The next day it was back to work for Kim, filling the long, lonely hours with concentrated polishing of antiques and studying in the library — anything to keep her mind off imagining what Neil might say when he arrived on Friday afternoon.

Two more clients arrived to keep her busy, and purchases were made. Kim's confidence soared anew as she began to realise how proficient she was becoming as a saleswoman.

Then there was her visit to Jake's studio, to see his wood carvings.

'Studio?' he grinned, embarrassed, as she reminded him of his invitation. 'Just an old shed, really. This way, Miss — I mean, Kim.'

She met his shy glance and smiled reassuringly, trying to put him at ease. 'I'm really looking forward to seeing your work, Jake. Have you always been interested in carving?'

He led the way to a large, wooden, shingle-tiled shed leaning against the far wall of the stable block, and Kim watched his rather melancholy face light up. 'Always loved it — ever since I was a boy. I used to whittle away when I should've been learning my lessons. That's why I'm a bit ignorant.

Couldn't get a better job.'

Kim felt warmth and commiseration fill her. Gently, she said, as he unlocked the door and stood aside to let her enter, 'We can't all be clever, Jake. Just think how dull the world would be if we were all the same . . . Oh!'

She didn't hear him close the door behind them, for she was completely taken aback by the sight which met her eyes. Shelves lined the long, thin shed, filled with wooden carvings, all expertly made.

Beside her stood a group of game dogs, the tension in their handsome bodies graphically illustrated. Farther down the shelf she saw more animals — horses, donkeys, and cats — all alive with that same magical quality of craftsmanship that had first taken her breath away.

Spellbound, she turned to him. 'Jake, they're marvellous!' And then, as he shook his head, mumbling something about it being just a hobby, she added quickly. 'No, I mean it.

They're so — alive. You sell them, of course?'

Jake passed by her and picked up a model cottage, looking down at it critically. 'No. Like I said, it's just a hobby.'

'Then you're a fool!' Kim's voice was sharp. 'Sorry, Jake, but honestly, these would fetch a huge price where I come from. I mean, models like this cost the earth in gift shops. You ought to take a few around — I know you'd get some orders.'

They looked at each other in the silence that followed. Kim saw that Jake was pleased, but nevertheless embarrassed. He turned away, replacing the model on the shelf, saying roughly, 'No, they're not good enough for that. But . . . ' Abruptly, he swung around, giving her his quick, nervous smile. 'But they're O.K. for presents. Maybe your boy would like one when he's here?'

Kim smiled warmly, realising that she'd said enough. This man wouldn't ever be pushed into doing things he considered unsuitable. She said quietly, 'Thanks, Jake. What a lovely thought. I know Roger would be thrilled to have one.'

He beamed and proudly showed her his work-bench, the neat racks of tools hanging above it and the beautifully-drawn blueprints of his next project — a model of Badlake House itself. Kim made a mental decision to have a private word with Neil Leston and ask if some of Jake's excellent work could not be displayed alongside the antiques.

However, she was soon to forget the idea, for suddenly it was Friday and she was thrown into turmoil, despite the calm front she presented as she prepared for Neil's week-end visit.

* * *

When at last he appeared, looking strained after the long drive from town, she had worked herself up into a state of near-panic. She opened the front door immediately as the car drew up, having spent most of the afternoon by the library window, trying to read a book on French porcelain.

She held her breath as Neil entered, smiling at her before flinging down the case and shrugging out of his coat.

'Hello, Kim,' he said casually. 'Don't mind if I call you Kim, do you? I'm Neil.'

His unexpected friendliness made it easier to mention what had been preying on her mind ever since his last phone call. 'No, I don't mind — but it's my surname that's the problem, isn't it?'

At the drawing-room door he paused, and turned to look back at her. She saw his eyes narrow, then he nodded.

'Look, give me a few moments to relax and change. It was one hell of a drive — so much fog. We'll talk over a cup of tea, right?'

Then the door shut and she went forlornly in to the kitchen to do as he'd asked. A little later, as she carried the loaded tray towards the drawing-room, she heard a call from farther down the passage.

'In here, Kim! Thought we'd be cosier in the study. The big room takes a day and a half to get warm in this weather.'

Surprised, she entered the study, putting the tray on the polished, oak table. Neil had lit the fire, already laid in the black, iron grate and it crackled welcomingly. Kim realised that the little room was much warmer and more comfortable than she had ever imagined it could be.

As she poured the tea, she glanced at the wall opposite, fancying the disapproving Victorian faces in the photographs were more friendly than they looked. The idea brought a half-smile to her taut face, but it faded as she handed Neil his tea, and then bent to put a silver dish of hot buttered crumpets on the hearth beside him.

He looked stern, almost put out, and although it was pleasant here in the study, she couldn't help being dismayed at the idea that he'd needed this privacy to say what he had to.

The tea scalded Kim's dry throat and she refused the crumpets. It was a relief when he looked across at her and said bluntly, 'I needed to talk to you. It's like this — Fiona kept on about recognising you.' He paused to replace his empty cup on the table, and Kim's heart lurched.

So she had been right. He and Fiona knew.

'She's got a cousin who's a journalist. I'm sure you can guess what happened . . .'

Kim met the impersonal stare and nodded numbly.

'Well' — Neil's voice displayed no emotion whatsoever — 'between them they raked up all the sordid details of the Bruce Hearne case, and there you were, for all the world to see — Bruce Hearne's wife, up on a murder charge.'

Suddenly, his expression changed, and Kim detected a definite hint of annoyance in his voice. 'Fiona's behaving rather badly, I'm afraid. She seems to have taken a dislike to you, and she threatened to tell everyone — particularly down here at Badlake — just who you are.'

Kim caught her breath. She stared bewilderedly at the man sitting opposite her in his winged armchair, stretching long legs to the warmth of the fire. Neil gave her a wry, brief flash of a smile.

'Well, actually we had quite a fight. I told her to keep quiet. She argued that everyone had a right to know. But, finally, I managed to persuade her to shut up.'

Persuade? wondered Kim hazily. She couldn't imagine Fiona being persuaded very easily. So they'd had a fight and over her.

She leaned forward in her straight-backed chair, the words pouring out of her in a jumble. 'I'm so sorry! So terribly sorry. I mean, bringing all this trouble on to you. But, once I'm gone, I'm sure it'll all blow over. I'll

107

go straight away . . . Pack up and leave tonight, catch the late train back to London. Back to Jess and Roger. Start again. Somewhere, somehow — '

'That's a load of nonsense. I won't hear of you going.

She stared, silenced by his peremptory tone. 'But — '

'No buts. Look here, Kim.' He, too, had leaned forward, holding her gaze across the hearth that divided them. 'All right, so you were involved in a very unpleasant case of murder. I won't pretend I wasn't shocked to realise you'd fooled me, but I can understand why you used a false name.'

'Not false. It's my — my maiden name.'

He smiled briefly. 'But false enough to make Fiona know that something wasn't right. God knows, she's like a terrier when she gets the scent, and nothing will stop her from digging and digging.'

Abruptly, his irritation disappeared, and he flashed a smile at Kim. 'I'm sorry for you. You've had a ghastly time, and I can imagine how wretched you must still feel.'

Something surged inside Kim, and in order to hide her feelings she snapped wildly, 'I don't need your pity, thanks. I've got on all right on my own so far, and I'll continue to do so.'

The brown eyes holding hers flared. Neil got to his feet and went to the window, staring out at the gathering dusk. When he finally spoke, his voice was even, showing no trace of the emotions she was certain her thoughtless words had aroused.

'I think you should reconsider your decision, Kim. You have a home here, and a job which you're starting to understand and do very well. You're going to be a great asset to me, and that's important. I've just told you that I've quietened Fiona's loose tongue, so there's no need for you to start running again. Why not stay here? You'll never get over this if you keep running, you know.'

In the silence that followed, Kim thought over the wise suggestion. He was right, of course. How foolish it had been of her to panic like that. If she went, how could she bear to be apart from Roger yet again?

In a low voice, she said meekly, 'Yes. Stupid of me. But I'm so used to running and hiding. I just thought — ' She sighed, despondent and exhausted. 'I'll stay. And thank you.'

★ ★ ★

'Tell me about Roger.' Neil's shadow fell over her and she looked up, to see him standing near her.

'My son. He's five. He's — ' She stopped and smiled wryly. 'He's the friend you said I could ask to stay.'

'And when is he coming?'

'Tomorrow afternoon. On the train.' Quickly she asked. 'Would you mind if I took the Capri?'

Neil gave her the full benefit of his smile. 'Of course not. But I've got a better idea. We'll drive up to the reference library. There's some research I have to do. Then we'll have lunch at the White Hart and meet your boy later. How does that suit you?'

Kim had no idea how to express her thanks. She stuttered, 'That's marvellous! Oh, thank you . . . ' Bewildered, she added, 'What research are you doing?' Then she bit her lip. 'Sorry! None of my business.'

Neil returned to the fireside. 'Research on the Leston family, actually. You see . . . ' Sitting down, he eyed her wearily. 'I'm compiling a family photograph album — trying to get together a sort of biography.'

Kim nodded, surprised at his friendliness. Daringly she inquired, 'But why are you doing it? Will you publish it?'

'Certainly not.' He paused. 'If you must know' — a suspicion of a smile took the tartness from his words — 'I'm doing it to try to get back the feeling of family bonds, ties, and responsibilities

111

which I lost when . . . ' Kim suddenly recalled what Mary Carew had told her, as he finished. ' . . . when my mother went off with another man, and my father died the following year. It hit me very hard.'

A silence followed as they both considered his words. Then Neil ran a hand through his dark hair and added almost ruefully, 'Funny, but I feel I can talk to you. Because you've suffered, too, I suppose.'

'Yes.' Almost shyly, Kim smiled, her recent terror and anger fading. 'And talking does one good — that's what I've found just lately.'

He nodded. 'So talk, Kim, if you want to, I'm listening.'

Taking a deep breath, she tried to marshal her thoughts. 'Well — when you talked about losing your family love, I remembered feeling the same. Only with me, it was my husband's love . . . '

The fire was reduced to a pale glow of dying embers, and through the uncurtained window dusk stole into the cosy little room, bringing shadows and an intimacy that made it possible for Kim to continue, painful though it was.

'You see, Bruce always wanted a daughter. And so, when Roger arrived — well, he wasn't exactly pleased.'

Neil's voice came softly out of the dimness. 'Most men long for a son.'

'Not Bruce.' Kim shut her eyes, to try to escape the cruel memories that suddenly sprang to mind. Hesitantly, she carried on. 'He took it out on Roger. At first, it was just not letting me pick him up when he cried. And then, as Roger got bigger, silly things like forgetting his birthday, or not keeping promises to play with him at the week-ends. Things that weren't too bad, although they upset Roger. And then — '

'And then?'

Kim clenched her hands as she said brokenly, 'And then Bruce decided that Roger must be punished when he was naughty.'

Across the room, Neil cleared his throat. 'Most kids need to be disciplined, you know.'

'But not like Bruce did! He was so strong. He didn't have to smack so hard — or lock Roger in his bedroom, to cry and cry . . .'

Kim couldn't go on until she felt a hand on her bowed shoulder and knew Neil stood behind her, sympathetic and interested. Somehow, he gave her the strength to continue, to get all the hatred and fear out of her system, where it had lain for so long.

'So Bruce started demanding that we have another baby. He said he was sure it would be a girl, next time . . .'

Her mind went back in time to their little London house, with Bruce just back from a successful fight in Birmingham. It had been a particularly gruelling evening, with Roger in tears and Bruce shouting and threatening. When, eventually, the uproar had subsided, Bruce had pulled her to him, as she went to make sure the back door was locked.

Even now, she could remember the whisky on his breath, hear his slurred voice as he tried to persuade her. 'C'mon, Kim, love. High time we had another — a lovely l'il girl. Kim? Kim!'

She'd pulled away, disgusted, her fear mounting rapidly. More than ever she'd begun to realise that beneath Bruce's charming facade, there hid a dark and violent stranger. He was a brute — yes, that was it exactly — a drunken, bullying, selfish brute.

* * *

Suddenly, Kim realised she'd been speaking her thoughts aloud. She caught her breath. She'd never meant to tell anyone, and certainly not the man whose hand still touched her shoulder and whose strength she felt infiltrating her taut, exhausted body. 'I — I'm sorry, Neil. I didn't mean to tell you.'

115

'Thank God you did. You needed to tell someone. So, how did it end?'

For a moment she felt unable to face any more of the memories. Catching her breath, she continued, 'I locked him out of my room. He ranted and raved, threatened to break the door down, and . . . ' Unconsciously, Kim touched her cheek. 'In the days that followed, he hit me — not just once, but on several occasions.'

The stark memory of the first time was there again. Bruce's massive hand knocking her against the door, and the pain sparking down her face. She remembered how grateful she'd been that Roger was out of the house, playing next door.

'Dear God!' Neil's shocked exclamation brought her back from the past.

She watched him return to his chair, and said, trying to smile, 'They were only bruises. But I knew then that I didn't love Bruce any more. In fact . . . ' She challenged the eyes that watched her so intently. 'In fact,

I knew then that if another man had wanted me, I would have gone. Just like that. Bruce and I were finished, you see.'

'But if you had gone, what would you have done about the boy? Would you have left Roger behind?'

Neil's blunt question seared through her as she cried, 'No!' But then she recalled how, later, and indeed just recently, she *had* left the boy behind. Did that make her an unnatural mother?

After a while, the silence which filled the darkened room grew oppressive. Kim stirred in her chair and Neil rose to switch on the light. Their eyes met across the room.

Feeling abject and foolish, Kim said slowly, 'I'd like to stay on here after all, Neil. You were right. I have a home and a job, so if it's still OK with you . . .'

'Of course,' he answered evenly and it seemed to Kim that he had retreated once again behind his own unassailable barrier. Perhaps she had offended him in some way.

'I told you I needed you here,' he said, breaking into her confusion. 'And clearly this is the right sort of place for someone in your position. Quiet. Remote. I mean, now that I've put paid to Fiona's little tricks it's hardly likely that anyone will find out who you are. Or what you did.'

His last words twisted like a knife inside her and she stared at him in stunned amazement. Despite the sympathy and understanding he'd offered, Neil was, in reality, simply offering a social misfit the chance to rehabilitate herself while at the same time performing a useful service for him.

'Thank you . . . ' It was pointless to say more. She should feel grateful that he considered it best for her to stay. Other employers would probably have been more heartless.

Rising, Kim went to the table and piled the empty cups on to the tray before leaving the study. Only when she was halfway through washing the dishes, did the reason for her depression and discontent dawn on her. She wanted Neil Leston to see her as a woman; not merely as a hopeless case.

★ ★ ★

Later that evening, alone in the cottage, Kim welcomed Jake's knock on the door. He had brought a toy for Roger, showing it to her with pride, and then smiling as she congratulated him on its beauty and his excellent craftsmanship.

'He'll love this, Jake. Will you stay for a coffee?'

The little wooden cat, carved so delicately that you could actually count the whiskers on its small, snub nose, sat on the mantelpiece as they chatted over coffee, with its original — Number Three warmly tucked up on Kim's lap.

The evening helped her regain her positive state of mind. She knew she was doubly lucky today; having Neil Leston as an employer and Jake as a friend.

However, her serenity was disturbed once again when, on going upstairs to fetch a photo of Roger to show Jake, she paused by the bedroom window after hearing footsteps on the gravel outside.

Neil was standing by the door. She watched him pick up something which leaned against the porch — Jake's stick with the carved dog's head. The stick was then replaced and in a few swift strides Neil was gone, heading back towards the house.

Kim was left feeling annoyed and disappointed. Had he come down especially to see her? Did he now think, perhaps, that she and Jake were becoming close — perhaps even closer than just good friends?

She drew the curtains and went downstairs. Life still seemed to have threats in store for her — would it never end?

Strangely, despite her uneasiness as she left the cottage next morning, the day turned out well. Neil was standing in a pool of sunlight, examining a camellia bush, as she came up the drive. Immediately he turned, giving her a friendly smile that banished her fears of the previous night.

'Morning. A beautiful one, too. I told you that the Moor wasn't always covered with a wet grey blanket, didn't I?'

And then, before she could do more than nod and smile briefly in exchange, he asked, 'You like flowers, don't you, Kim? I saw you'd put one of these in the study. Reminded me of my mother — she always picked the first buds in March . . . '

His face, Kim noted with surprise and pleasure, looked unusually relaxed and carefree. She watched as he turned back to the bush, fingering the dark, glossy leaves with gentle hands, and bending to smell the fragrance of the pale petals. A shadow of doubt eased out of her mind. No man who cared for nature like this could be as hard and careless as she had suspected Neil Leston of being yesterday afternoon.

'I'm glad you noticed,' she said impulsively. 'I thought that poor, sad study needed cheering up. Amid all those serious faces it's something to smile at.'

Thoughtfully, Neil nodded without speaking, as if some small problem had just been satisfactorily resolved. 'And you were right, of course.' The words were accompanied by a flash of that same expression which had persuaded her to confide in him.

Kim's own smile broadened, and her heartbeat grew faster. Sunshine and the prospect of Roger coming home, coupled with the fact that Neil was pleased with her, helped to chase away the old pain and anguish. She went into the house almost gaily, his last words floating after her.

'I'll get the car round and then we'll be off. OK, Kim?'

She turned and nodded, a broad smile lighting up her face. It was so long since a man had looked at her as Neil had just done.

The drive to Exeter was full of talk and friendly silences. Neil pointed out places of interest, and Kim's mind was kept so busy that she had no time for any more introspection.

When the city opened up around them, she could only think of how much longer it would be before Roger's train arrived. Somehow she controlled her impatience and enjoyed an hour exploring the shops while Neil disappeared into the library. They met later at the entrance to the White Hart.

'Did you find what you wanted?' she asked as they sat in the bar having a drink before lunch. Neil nodded, and she saw a gleam of what might have been excitement in his eyes.

'More than I bargained for, in fact. I

got some information about my great-uncle who went to war with the Devon Regiment and became something of a local hero. Fascinating, isn't it? To think of what went on before my parents were born . . . '

'And all this will go in your book?' Kim sipped her Martini, more than ever attracted by the new Neil she was seeing on this unexpectedly lovely day.

'You bet it will! Ah, our table's ready — let's go, shall we? All that brain work's made me hungry.'

And now, at last, they were at the station. Kim could no longer control herself, running madly up the platform as the train drew in, her head craning to peer in at every window in search of Roger. Where was he? Surely nothing had gone wrong? But why couldn't she see him?

'Mum!'

Kim turned, her heart in her mouth, and rushed towards the small figure standing beside a large canvas bag, right at the far end of the station.

'Roger! Darling.'

She swept him into her arms, hardly hearing his excited chatter, knowing only that he was here at last, they were together, and nothing — but nothing — would ever part them again.

Roger wriggled away, clutching comics and a half-empty bag of crisps, and tugged at her hand. 'Let's say good-bye to Ken,' he urged with enthusiasm.

Kim had to laugh or she would have cried. 'Who's Ken?'

'The guard! He's great. Over here, Mum!'

By the time Kim had thanked the man, she suddenly realised that she had left Roger's luggage on the platform. Turning, she nearly bumped into Neil, who was standing watching, and holding the bag in his hand. She pulled Roger away from Ken's friendly farewell and presented him to Neil.

'This is Roger. Darling, say hello to Mr Leston, who said you could come and stay.'

Just for a moment she saw Roger's

face fall. He stood back, looking lonely and defensive, and she knew, with a lurch of her stomach, that he was remembering Bruce. Bruce, who would play one moment, and hit out the next.

'Darling, it's all right. I promise.'

The little boy looked up at her, saw the reassurance on her face, then obediently lifted his bright, red head to meet Neil's smile.

'Hi, Roger. Had a good trip?' Neil bent down and shook the boy's hand.

It dawned hazily on Kim that, family man or not, he certainly had the knack of being able to talk to a child without being patronising.

Roger beamed happily. 'You bet! Ken showed me the brakes and the guard's van and everything. And he bought me a Coke!'

'Great. Well, let's go home, shall we?' Neil stood up, the boy's hand in his, and led the way up the platform towards the exit.

'H — home?'

Kim's eyes flew from Roger's puzzled face to Neil's. 'The cottage where you'll be living with your mum,' he said quietly. 'And tomorrow you can come and see my home, which is bigger, and not so cosy as yours.'

'Have you got a car?' Roger demanded, as they stepped out of the station. Kim, amused, saw how his eyes widened as Neil went up to the shining Porsche parked opposite. 'Phew! What is it?'

Neil opened the door. '1986 Porsche. And in London I use a little red Sprite — easy to park, and zips through the traffic.'

'Cor!' Roger was suitably impressed. After that, there was no holding his enthusiasm. He jumped into the waiting car, plying Neil with questions as they drove back towards Dartmoor. Kim sitting next to him on the roomy, front seat listened to her son and Neil, and thought of how long it had been since she'd known such happiness.

Then, gradually, Roger's excited

conversation died away. He put his head on Kim's shoulder and slept. Gently, Kim lifted him on to her lap, and saw Neil's sidelong grin as she did so.

They drove the rest of the way in companionable silence. Neil dropped them off at the cottage, and as soon as the car stopped, Roger was awake.

'Is this it? Is this home? Let me get out, Mum

Neil carried the bag to the door and said quietly to Kim as she found the key, 'Have the rest of the day to yourselves. No need to come up to the house.' Nodding firmly, he went back to the car, grinning as whoops of joy sounded from inside the cottage.

'Mum! There's a cat here!'

Desperately, Kim wanted to express her gratitude. She followed Neil to the car and said unevenly, 'Look, I don't know how to say this — but you've made everything so wonderful. Well, thanks.'

The dark eyes searched her own for

a moment, then Neil said casually, 'It's been a pleasure. Young Roger is a great kid — a credit to you. Look, I'll see you both tomorrow — OK?'

She nodded dumbly, and watched the car back away and disappear up the drive. Unfortunately, her state of mindless euphoria couldn't last — Roger flew out of the cottage, sucking his fingers and howling. 'That beastly cat! Look what it's done — I've got bloody fingers!'

Kim hugged him to her, kissing away the tears. 'Come on in, darling,' she coaxed. 'I can see you and Number Three have got to be properly introduced! He's a country cat, and he won't understand your London ways. Now, gently does it, my love . . . '

The evening slid past in a welter of talk, plans, and shared affection. By the time Roger was finally tucked up, in the little attic bedroom beneath the sloping eaves, Kim was tired out. And, although she meant to make various plans and schemes before going to sleep, no sooner had her head touched the pillow than she was away, her last conscious thought being gratitude for such a wonderful day.

★ ★ ★

It was lunchtime the following morning before Kim or Roger knew it. There had been so much to do.

'Do I have to come in? I've just found this spade — I want to dig the garden.' Roger already looked like a country child, thought Kim. His wellingtons were muddy, the dark blue sweater trailed a long thread after being snagged on a bramble as he defied the wilderness of the garden, and best of all, to her adoring eyes, his cheeks were bright pink. It seemed that the pure Dartmoor air had already changed him from the pale, London child into a sturdy, little boy.

'We'll come out again after lunch, darling. I'll help you. Shall we use those stones to make a rockery?'

'Oh, yes, Mum!'

They were engrossed in their work when, later, footsteps came crunching down the drive, stopping outside the cottage. Roger looked up first, letting out a yell of delight.

'It's Neil!' He went flying off to meet his new friend and Kim straightened up, suddenly conscious of her shabby jeans and wind-blown hair.

She called after him, 'You mean Mr Leston, Roger!' Then she saw Neil grin and shake his head as he withstood the boy's boisterous welcome.

'Neil's fine. We're friends.'

Kim watched, amazed at the way the two got on. Roger was being handled just right, treated as an equal, but quietly corrected if his natural exuberance got out of hand.

'How about a cup of tea? Roger and I have been heaving these stones about for hours,' Kim offered.

Neil nodded cheerfully. 'Sounds good. We'll finish this pile while you get it ready.'

'Crumpets, Mum?' Roger had always loved his food.

Kim ruffled his carroty hair as she passed. 'Crumpets, you greedy creature. And make sure you take off those filthy boots before you come in.'

They all sat around the fire as the evening slowly drew in, and Kim once again wondered at the contentment which was so evident in the little room. Tea was finished, the kitten had been petted and played with, Jake's present admired, and now Roger sat on the floor at Neil's feet, watching as Neil drew pictures for him.

The room was warm, and Kim began to feel drowsy as she relaxed, enjoying the homeliness and affection that surrounded her. Then there was the swish of car wheels outside. Someone was beating an imperious tattoo with the brass knocker on the cottage door. Kim's joy died instantly, replaced by the old knot of anxiety and fear.

'I'll go.' She got up, telling herself not to be silly. It was probably only

Jake, coming to meet Roger. But Jake had no car. Perhaps it was Mary Carew, checking up on the kitten.

But the face that confronted her as she opened the door wasn't as welcome as either of the visitors she had half-expected to see.

Fiona smiled triumphantly. 'Ah! Mrs Hearne, I believe?'

Wretchedly, Kim just stared. 'Miss Cartwright. Come in, won't you?' Not that she wanted this woman in her home, but what else could she do?

Fiona entered, her quick, exploratory gaze immediately settling on Neil, whose face was suddenly set and cold.

'Thought I might find you here, darling. Jake said you'd gone out. But what on earth are you doing, Neil? Playing happy families or something?'

Neil's voice was blunt. 'Visiting friends, Fiona, that's what.'

Kim hovered in the doorway, watching the confrontation and seeing, too, how Roger sat up on the floor and also watched.

Although she was uneasy at Fiona's visit, Kim's main concern now was for the boy's welfare. She hoped against hope that Fiona would say nothing to upset him.

But she hoped in vain. Fiona stood face-to-face with Neil, clearly gloating over the quarrel she was forcing him into. Her voice was sweet and rich, and made the fearsome words she uttered next sound even more depraved and horrific.

'Darling, you don't choose your friends very wisely, do you? I mean, this woman's a murderess! Hadn't you better watch out that you're not her next victim?'

5

An ominous silence followed Fiona's terrible question, and Kim felt herself go rigid with horror. Thoughts raced through her mind. Did Neil really see her as a murderess? Did he actually think she might kill again?

It was a return of her old nightmare, made even worse by Roger's presence. Suddenly, Kim thought of what her small son had heard Fiona say. With a huge effort she steadied herself and took a deep breath, bending down to put a protective arm around the little boy's shoulders.

'Darling, run upstairs and play, will you?' she whispered.

But he was staring up at her his eyes confused, and she knew it was too late to try to shield him from this awful moment.

'Mum, what's a — a murderess?' he

asked in a high, trembling voice. Kim closed her eyes as she hugged him to try to blot out the pain which the question caused.

'Just a funny name, darling . . . ' It was hard to keep her voice steady.

'Oh.' She felt him relax a little as he asked, 'Like a nickname?'

'Something like that.'

And then she was aware of a movement beside her as Neil abruptly leaped up, heading for the doorway, his right hand raised as if ready to strike Fiona. Again, her stomach twisted with dismay for this was the worst thing that could happen with Roger watching — he would remember Bruce's violence.

Hardly knowing what she was doing, Kim followed Neil across the room, grasping his arm as he confronted Fiona in the doorway. 'No! No! Please don't, Neil.'

The anguish in her voice made him pause and look back at her. He was white with anger, but she realised thankfully it was not directed at her. Quickly, she turned to Fiona, feeling her own rage bubble up anew as she recalled Roger's frightened reaction.

'Look, let me explain. It wasn't really that way at all. Not' — She paused, finding it almost impossible to force out the dreadful word, but finally she did so — 'Not murder . . . but manslaughter.'

Fiona still smiled, but her eyes held no warmth. She shrugged. 'A different name for the same crime. I mean, you still killed him, didn't you?'

Kim was at her wit's end. Turning away from the lovely, sneering face, she looked helplessly at Neil, noticing that he was in control of himself again.

As their eyes met, he gave her a long, hard look and touched her hand briefly. 'Don't be upset. We'll talk it out later.' Then he went over to Roger, pulling the child to his feet. 'Want a ride in my nice new Porsche?' he asked cheerfully, and Kim felt her throat tighten as all Roger's worries disappeared.

'Oooh, yes, please!' He looked up at Neil adoringly, then glanced towards Kim. 'I don't have to go to bed yet, Mum, do l?'

'No, darling, not for a bit.'

'I'll bring him back when he's forgotten about all this.' Neil's quiet words were for her ears only, and she nodded, unable to speak. She watched as he took the boy out of the cottage, walking past Fiona as if she were not there.

But Fiona was not to be treated so casually. 'Neil! What the hell are you playing at?' Her smile had vanished and her eyes were ablaze.

Neil's voice floated back through the open doorway. 'Not playing, Fiona — just trying to repair the damage you've caused.'

In the porch, Fiona watched as the two figures tramped off up the drive, Roger happily looking up at his tall companion and chattering as they went. Slowly, she turned to meet Kim's smouldering stare.

'Well! Looks as if your dirty little wiles have worked once again. You've got Neil under your thumb, haven't you? But don't think I can't get him out again . . .'

Kim was trembling, but her voice remained steady as she answered quietly. 'All I care about is keeping Roger safe and happy. It doesn't matter what filth you throw at me. I'm past being hurt any more.' Yet, even as the brave words came out, she wondered how true they were.

She and Fiona stared at each other for a few seconds until Fiona was the first to drop her eyes. Grudgingly, she muttered, 'I didn't mean to upset the boy. I didn't even know he was here.' And then, with a smirk, her unpleasantness flared again. 'I suppose you persuaded soft old Neil to let you bring him down here?'

'No!' Kim's voice rang out sharply. 'I did no such thing. I hate asking favours — even for my son. It was Neil who suggested I had someone here to keep me company. And he seemed to welcome Roger . . . '

Fiona laughed unkindly. 'I'm afraid you've got the wrong ideas about darling Neil. He's no family man. He hated his own parents and he can't stand children, so don't bank on him becoming your boy's protector. All Neil is interested in are his precious antiques, his profits — and me.'

The lovely face was smiling again, so sure of itself. Kim moved away, aware of a tremor of fear running down her spine.

Surely this woman was devoid of all warmth and understanding? It struck Kim that even she, a 'murderess', had never been so cold and forbidding as Fiona Cartwright was now showing herself to be.

She stepped back into the cottage, knowing she could stand no more. 'Good-bye, Miss Cartwright,' she muttered, and shut the door in Fiona's surprised and furious face.

Alone, Kim searched for some task that would keep her distraught mind from exploring anew all that had just happened. She tidied the room that had suddenly become cold and empty, then made up the dying fire. Neil would soon bring Roger home and they would have to talk.

A black cloud of dread began to build up inside her. Neil would insist on knowing exactly what had happened between her and Bruce. Dumbly, she acknowledged that she owed it to him to tell the truth. He had been so wonderful, standing up for her, protecting Roger, and even confronting his own fiancée. She knew the time had come to tell him just what had happened between Bruce and her. But how was she to put that devastating and traumatic event into words?

Suddenly they were back. She heard a car outside, Roger's piping voice, and then the two of them were pushing

141

open the door and standing there, smiling at her.

Roger babbled excitedly as he rushed over to hug her. 'We drove on a private road, and I sat on Neil's lap and steered! And he says I can do it again, next time he's here . . . '

Over her son's dishevelled red head, Kim met Neil's gaze and saw a mixture of emotions on his face. There was obvious amusement at Roger, but underneath the smile she knew that his anger still smouldered. She wouldn't like to be Fiona, facing Neil in this mood.

With new perception, Kim realised that not all men were violent, as Bruce had been. Neil, in anger, would use words and not blows. And then she remembered that he had said they would talk it out later. Kim felt herself shrink, as she guessed the moment had arrived.

Neil interrupted her thoughts, asking, 'Will you be OK for the night? The boy's tired out, I think. And you, will you sleep?' It was with a surge of relief that she answered, almost inaudibly, 'Yes. Oh, yes.'

'Then I'll be on my way. Fiona's waiting for me up at the house, I . . . ' For a second she saw his face twist and caught her breath as he added, 'Sorry I can't stay, Kim, but — '

'I understand. It's all right. We'll be fine.'

His face cleared as he turned back to the open door and said formally, 'Good night, then. We'll talk tomorrow, once I've made Fiona return to town.' Unexpectedly, he looked over his shoulder, and his voice grew suddenly warmer. 'I think we need to be truthful with each other, Kim — don't we?'

Without waiting for an answer, he smiled briefly at Roger. 'Good night, my lad, and don't give your mum any trouble — OK?'

Roger's grin persisted while he listened to the door close and the car crunch away. Then he turned back to Kim, threw himself on her lap, and said in his most persuasive voice, 'I'm ever so hungry, Mum. Can I have chips for supper?'

As she stood at the cooker ten minutes later, hearing vigorous splashing from the bathroom upstairs, Kim shut her eyes and silently blessed Neil for his help with Roger. She was almost sure that the unpleasant scene, and Fiona's words, were safely forgotten now.

But once Roger was asleep, the evening became unbearable, and she felt on edge as never before. Above all, she recalled Neil's last demand, that they must talk tomorrow, and her whole body became chilled at the thought of facing him and trying to relive that last ghastly scene with Bruce. No. She could never make herself go through with it.

* * *

Very early the next morning, after a restless, haunted night, Kim suggested a walk on the moor to Roger.

His eyes shone in happy anticipation. 'Can we have a picnic? Got any crisps, Mum?'

Kim smiled weakly, and thanked God for his healthy appetite. 'I'll see what I can find — you and your prawn-flavoured crisps! Look, you'd better wear your wellies and your anorak.'

They were away from the cottage well before the village church, half a mile away, echoed distantly at nine o'clock. The day was sharp, for all its clearness and beauty, and Kim was glad they both wore thick sweaters. However, the exercise soon made her glow, and she looked down with contentment at Roger's pink ears sticking out from beneath his blue, woolly hat.

'This is great, Mum!' He strode out, obviously intent on getting his boots as wet as possible in every patch of bog that they encountered. Sometimes racing ahead of her, occasionally falling behind to examine a flower half-hidden in the heather, Roger plodded on happily.

Kim's fear and panic slowly began to subside as they turned off along a narrow lane, signed simply, 'To the Moor'. Who would concentrate on mere personal problems in such a dominating landscape?

Dartmoor was all around them, still and remote, the silence a vital part of its attraction and mystery. A pony whinnied in the bracken, a lark ascended, trilling, and the wind blew gently.

So it was true, Kim thought with a stab of realisation, all that she had heard about this place. Beautiful, wild, lonely — yet filled with a sense of peace.

★ ★ ★

They were now approaching a track leading off the unfenced lane and she began to hurry. She needed to leave civilisation for a short while, to be alone and carefree. Somehow she knew that out there, in the middle of the wilderness, her mind would stop striving and she would discover how best to say all that she had to when next she saw Neil.

A screech of brakes turned her head back to the lane, instinctively she pulled Roger to her. Mary Carew looked out of the open window of her elderly, mud-splashed Land-Rover, and smiled as she called, 'You're a couple of early birds! Taking a morning constitutional?'

Kim smiled back, but paused before replying. 'That's it,' she said finally. 'We couldn't resist the sunshine. Roger, say hello to Mrs Carew.'

Kim watched Mary as she grinned at the boy and asked, 'Are you and the kitten good friends yet?'

Roger nodded, his eyes sparkling.

'You must come over to the stables one day and meet all the other animals,' Mary said before driving on. 'Cheerio for now. Have a good walk.'

He turned to Kim quickly. 'Can I go? She's nice, isn't she?'

'Of course you can, love. And yes,

she's very nice indeed.'

As they walked on, Kim reflected grimly that if only Fiona hadn't dropped her bombshell last night, life here at Badlake could have been a contented one. She had made new friends — three of them — and had a job, a home, and Roger living with her. If only Fiona had kept quiet.

Kim was so caught up in her thoughts that she was soon unaware of which way they were headed, or of the distance they were covering. It was Roger's weary voice that pulled her back to reality, after they had been walking, unknown to her, for a good hour and a half.

'Mum, I'm hungry. Let's have our picnic.'

Startled, she came back to the reality of the wilderness stretching all around them. The hills, brown, green, and tinged here and there with purple, enclosed them. Not far away, white blobs of flowers swung and swayed in the wind, and it was only as her

148

boots squelched into bright green bog that sucked and clung, did Kim realise the moor was not all peace and beauty. On her first day here, Neil had warned her about straying off the track because of bogs.

Kim cursed her stupidity at not having taken a note of landmarks as they walked. Uneasily, she realised that out here everything looked the same. As she forced herself to chatter encouragingly to Roger, she wondered how she would find the way home again after their picnic.

But sitting on the heather-clad slopes of a small stream, sharing sandwiches with Roger and enjoying his laughter as they threw twigs into the fast, brown waters, she forgot her fears. The sun was warm, and Dartmoor was surely the most beautiful place she had ever known.

'How are your feet, love?' she asked, as Roger kicked off his boots and sat on a granite boulder, dabbling his toes in the stream.

'A bit sore.' He grinned at her, then added stoutly. 'But I'll be OK. It's always quicker going home, isn't it, Mum?'

Nodding, she prayed silently that he was right. 'Let's have a little rest first — just for ten minutes, and then we'll be really fresh and it won't seem any distance at all. Come on, let's cuddle down here on my anorak, out of the wind . . .'

Although he fidgeted for a few minutes, Roger soon fell asleep, but despite her sudden weariness, Kim was unable to follow his example. Once again as she closed her eyes, she was back in the life she had shared with Bruce, before the horror of that last, mind-shattering scene.

★ ★ ★

She recalled that as Bruce's fame grew throughout the world of professional boxing, she had tried to come to a decision about leaving him or not. She

150

had gone through such agony of mind during this time, and Bruce had been little help.

'You're always miserable nowadays, Kim. What's got into you? Here I am, going places — earning money, making a name for myself, and all you can do is stay at home like a wet week-end. What's up, eh?'

She had looked at him that night, as they ate a sumptuous meal in a well-known London restaurant, and felt that she was sitting opposite a stranger. Something told her that the truth would only provoke yet another ugly scene, and so she searched for words that would make him understand, but at the same time knowing dully that it wasn't possible.

'It's hard for me to come to terms with your fame, Bruce. I mean — everything is different now. *You're* different.'

'You're damn right!' He guffawed and looked around, waiting for a show of recognition from nearby tables. 'I'm a household name after winning that fight with Tiger Meadway at Wembley . . . of course I'm different! I'm enjoying life now. This is what I've always wanted.'

He leaned over the table, his eyes eager and slightly glazed with drink. 'So why can't you enjoy it, too? Talk about a long face! Cheer up! Don't I give you nice presents? Clothes? Holidays? What about that gold bracelet, eh?'

Fingering the chunky clasp around her wrist, Kim nodded, smiling pleadingly at him as she did so. 'Yes, it's lovely, and it was sweet of you, Bruce. You're so generous — but — ' Suddenly she gathered up her courage. 'But we're hardly ever together now. You travel so much. We're growing apart. Maybe if we had more time together, like we used to, then maybe we'd be — well — happier.'

'Happier?' His smile died instantly, replaced by a look of annoyance which marred his handsome face, and made him childishly petulant. 'What's that supposed to mean? I'm happy enough — so why aren't you?'

Suddenly, Kim saw his fury flare. His voice grew louder, and he refilled his wine glass with a fierce movement. 'You're a proper misery, Kim! You and that whining kid, you make my life hell! And after all I've done for you, all I give you — '

'I only want us to be happy like we used to be.' Kim was trembling, knowing that he was rapidly losing control. In a minute he'd be shouting, trying to grab her across the table, and making yet another scene to fill the gutter Press tomorrow morning. Oh, God, she thought, is it always going to be like this? Rows and violence and unhappiness for the rest of our lives? What's to become of us? Of me, Bruce, and Roger?

Then his big hand grabbed hers and she was yanked off her chair and dragged through the restaurant, his shouted, rude complaints filling her ears and shaming her because of the commotion he was causing. Heads turned, and a buzz of comment followed them. Waiters appeared, and there was an argument as Bruce flung down the money to settle the bill.

Outside, in the foyer, a camera flashed, and Kim, following Bruce blindly out to a waiting cab, heard a man say grimly, 'Wow! Bruce Hearne on the warpath again. Front page tomorrow, I guess. But I wouldn't be in his poor wife's shoes — not for anything.'

★ ★ ★

At that point, merciful sleep put an end to her agonised memories and when she awoke, some fifty minutes later, she was all too aware of the present to give any more thought to the past.

She was alone, and there was no sight or sound of Roger. At first Kim couldn't think where she was, and then the silence, broken only by the cold blustering wind and the nearby chuckle of running water, brought her back to reality.

Sunshine still poured down, but its warmth had gone, and when she looked up at the sky she saw a cluster of grey clouds racing towards her from the horizon. The beauty of the moorland still made her catch her breath, but now something else was present in the solitude — a sense of menace.

Kim leaped to her feet, staring all around her. It was silly to be so frightened — Roger had only gone out of sight for a moment. He was probably looking for fish around the bend of the stream — or climbing the grey rocks that crowned the nearby hillside. She had only to call and he would answer, waving, full of glee, his bright face bringing her joy and reassurance.

'Roger! Roger!' Her shouts were snatched away by the hustling wind. And in the encircling panorama of green and brown hillside, nothing stirred. Kim felt a hint of panic rise within her. Suddenly she forgot the beauty of the moor and instead became frighteningly aware of its darker side. Oh, God, what a fool she had been to come all this way and to let Roger wander off.

Despairingly, she raced towards the rock-clad tor in the distance and started climbing, shouting as she went. Breathless, she reached the top, willing herself to look down from the windswept heights and praying she would see a small figure plodding back towards her. But there was nothing, save a herd of wandering ponies grazing in the bracken, some half mile away.

Kim was becoming frantic. By now the sun was beginning to sink in the afternoon sky, and the day would soon be coming to an end. She *must* find Roger before darkness fell.

'Roger!' Again, her call faded into the wind and, despite the heat of her body after the hard climb up the tor, she shivered. Dartmoor was a terrible place — impersonal and ageless. How could she ever have thought it peaceful and lovely? Leaving the rocks behind her, she climbed down the hillside, her desperation mounting. What was she to do? Which way should she go? Where else could she look? Oh, Roger, where are you?

And then, as she stumbled on, not knowing which direction to take, another name came to mind, and she cried aloud in her anguish. 'Neil! For God's sake, help me, Neil!' But how could he? He didn't even know she was here. And if he did know — would he care?

It seemed to Kim that she had been running and searching for hours on end. The light was fading by the time she came to a halt by some rocks. Resting against them to get her breath back, she noticed something being blown across her line of vision.

She fell on it with a sob of gratitude. It was Roger's empty crisp packet. It must be his, she thought as she read the lettering — 'prawn-flavoured crisps'. She must be on the right track after all. Her mind grew clearer and she began to feel more optimistic. She would find him, of course she would. Any minute now.

But as she ploughed on, her anxiety soon returned. The land was sloping downwards and ahead of her lay a seemingly impassable patch of bog. The white, cotton-shaped flowers stood up like warning flags, and she picked her way nervously around the edge of the morass. Had Roger come this way? Supposing he had gone straight on into the bog . . .

No, surely he would remember getting his boots stuck earlier this morning and avoid it. Kim ran on and suddenly, around a cleft in the hillside, again found the stream by which they had picnicked. Now the waters boiled and surged as they raced over the stony bed of the small chasm, all charm and friendliness gone. Spray made the bordering boulders slippery, and Kim crossed them with great care, some instinct making her follow the stream as it thundered downwards.

And then she saw him. He was lying in a crumpled heap just ahead of her, at the bottom of a long, sloping rock which stopped short of the tumbling waters. She guessed he must have tried climbing the rocks, only to fall after slipping on the wet moss at the water's edge. He lay very still, and Kim's heart leaped in fear.

'Roger!' Somehow, with hands and knees grazed in the process, she reached him, and kneeled by his side.

'Mum!' He was crying, but his face cleared the minute he saw her. Kim hugged him silently and he let out a whimper of pain. 'Ow! My leg!'

Kim comforted him. 'You're all right, love. I'll get you home, don't worry. Thank God you're safe, my darling!'

But even as she held him close and then gently eased off one boot to look at his twisted leg, Kim wondered how she could possibly make her words come true. Clearly the boy wasn't able to walk and it looked as if his ankle was badly sprained. Swollen and discoloured already with bruising it was far too painful to bear his weight.

'I can't walk, Mum,' he said as he bravely tried to stand upright. With the boy balancing precariously on his good leg. Kim somehow managed to help him get down from the rock overlooking the rushing water.

'Then I'll carry you!'

But Kim soon discovered that Roger was all bone and muscle as he wound his arms around her neck.

'We'll do — a few steps — at a time.' She smiled reassuringly at his white, stricken face and tried to ease his shock and pain by talking as she struggled along. 'Tell me why you went off? Why didn't you wake me up?'

'It was the ponies. They came up to drink. You were so fast asleep that you didn't even hear them. They looked so pretty, I wanted to stroke them and give them some of my crisps. But as soon as I got near they went away. And I didn't know how far I'd gone.

When I looked around I couldn't see you any more . . . and then I found that waterfall and thought it'd be fun to try to jump across — it wasn't very wide . . . '

Kim shivered at the thought. How easily he could have fallen into the tumbling waters and been thrown against the cruel rocks . . .

'But I slipped and fell down that big stone and got my foot stuck at the bottom. Oh, Mum can't you go faster? I want to go home!'

'So do I, my love. Crumpets and a cup of tea would be nice, wouldn't they?' She sounded calm, but inwardly Kim felt nothing but despair.

The sun was rapidly disappearing and it was getting so cold. She knew she would not be able to carry Roger much farther, she was too weak, too unused to such demands on her frail strength. Again her thoughts drifted and Neil's name was on her lips. Oh, Neil, if only you could help me now . . .

'What's that building over there, Mum? See, at the side of those trees? Looks like a falling-down house or something.'

Putting him down for a moment, she stared at the huddle of sycamore trees in the dip of ground where Roger was pointing, and a surge of hope shot through her. 'Let's go and see.'

Maybe it would shelter them from the approaching night. Carefully, she heaved Roger on to her back, piggy-back fashion, and stumbled down towards the pile of fallen stones and the encircling trees.

'It must have been a farm once. Look, there's a fireplace there and what's left of a window.'

The ruin was unwelcoming and wretched, but behind its crumbling walls she gently laid Roger on the bare ground, taking off her anorak to act as a blanket. He seemed cold and drowsy and she forced herself to be bright as she foraged in the picnic bag, finding what remained of their meal.

'Aren't you the lucky one? Half a tin of Coke and a chocolate biscuit!'

He managed a feeble grin and sat up, wincing. 'What about you, Mum?'

'Oh, I'm not a bit hungry, thanks, love.' She sat down beside him, close enough to keep off the wind which came whistling around the wall. The ground was chill, and the stones behind them seemed even colder.

Trying hard to make herself forget her own discomfort, Kim chattered on to Roger and was rewarded by feeling the little body eventually sag against her as he slept. Only then did she force her own shivering body to relax, as she bleakly faced the wretched situation.

They were lost on the moor — no longer could she escape the fact. No one knew they were here and, even if she could carry Roger farther, she had no map, no compass, and the night was coming down fast. Kim bowed her head and she knew that she had been a fool to come out so unprepared and ignorant.

She was shivering uncontrollably now. If only she had worn thicker clothes. If only she had taken advice about the moor before starting out. If only Neil was here . . .

Despairingly, she tried to sleep, but the peaceful daytime silence was now broken by frightening noises. The wind began to howl around the ruined walls and something scurried and rustled, startling her ever further. And then she awoke out of a troubled, light sleep to hear another sound.

An animal's paws were scraping on the stones nearby, and a shadowy shape suddenly bounded over the wall to stand, panting beside her, a wet nose nuzzling her trembling hand. Kim felt she might die of fright, until the creature whined and then she realised.

'Brutus! Oh Brutus, you clever, wonderful dog you've found us! Jake must be here!' Kim leaped to her feet and stared into the darkness. Then she heard voices, faint and indistinct through the wind, but human, thank God.

'Kim! Are you there? Kim!'

Jake and Mary appeared in the wavering glow of a lantern and Kim collapsed thankfully in Mary's arms. 'Oh, thank God you've found us! It's Roger he's hurt his leg — and I was so afraid — '

Jake, warm and reassuring, wrapped his jacket around her and pulled her close to him, 'Relax, Kim. Everything's all right now. We'll get the boy out of here in no time. Look, Mrs Carew's got a flask of hot soup.'

* * *

In that wonderful moment a burden slipped from Kim's aching shoulders — she wasn't alone anymore. But, as both she and Roger thankfully sipped the soup and ate the sandwiches that Mary had also produced, she felt a stab of dismay. Where was Neil? Did he know what had happened? Did he know — and not care?

Her thoughts were interrupted by Mary, hustling her along out of the ruins towards two pinpoints of light in the near distance. 'That's the Range Rover, only a step now, and Jake's got Roger on his back. Before you know it, my dear, you'll be safe and at home again.'

The Range Rover, Kim knew, belonged to Neil — did that mean he was there, after all? The thought brought a new strength into her weary legs and a glow to her body. But when at last the big vehicle came into sight, Neil had no welcome for her.

He simply said curtly. 'So you're all right. Well, thank God for that.'

Then he went past her to help Jake with his precious burden and get Roger into the back of the Range Rover with Mary beside him.

Kim was squashed on to the front seat between Jake and Neil as they drove back through the night to the nearest hospital, nine miles away.

There, she sat in an overheated waiting-room while Neil stayed with Roger, who was being treated in casualty.

Mary brought her some coffee from the vending machine and said reassuringly, 'I don't suppose the boy's leg will be much trouble, kids are always getting into scrapes.'

But Kim felt too shocked and exhausted to be hopeful. 'Thank goodness you saw us setting off,' she said. 'Oh, God, I feel so ashamed of myself . . . '

Mary's warmth died for a moment. 'And so you should be. Neil was on the verge of calling out the Dartmoor Rescue team before he thought to ring me. Luckily, I knew more or less where you'd been heading because I'd seen you starting off. But it was actually Jake who suggested we should try ruined Teignhead Farm — and good old Brutus took it from there.' She looked at Kim ruefully, as a smile eased her sharp expression. 'You were damned lucky, my girl, and I hope you realise it.'

'I do. Oh, I do . . . ' Kim nodded wretchedly, and suddenly Mary's arm was around her shoulders.

'The lecture's over, love. Try to cheer up — it could have turned out much worse, you know.'

And then, suddenly, Neil was at the door with a grinning Roger supported by him and Jake. 'The lad had VIP treatment, arriving at this hour! The entire staff turned out to give him the once-over! They've plastered his ankle, it wasn't a sprain but a hair-fracture. Oh, don't worry, it'll heal quite easily within weeks. So let's get home, shall we? Come on, my lad — Jake and I will give you a lift back to the Range Rover.'

Kim was past caring about anything as, once again, she climbed up between Neil and Jake and was driven through winding lanes to Badlake House. Exhaustion and shock had caught up with her, and she only nodded dumbly as Neil said firmly that she and Roger must stay for the night and until such time as the plaster was removed.

'You won't be able to manage with him at the cottage, so you can stay up here. Oh, it's no trouble,' he assured her as she opened her mouth to try to thank him. 'Just try to get some sleep. I think we could all do with some rest now.' His face was set and he offered no smiling reassurance.

Kim undressed and got into the huge four-poster bed, where Roger already lay, with a feeling of dread niggling her troubled mind.

Things had gone from bad to worse. Neil must think her a complete idiot now, as well as a woman with an unsavoury past. She closed her eyes, miserably aware that the morning must inevitably bring with it the long-awaited and feared confrontation between them.

★ ★ ★

As she had expected, Neil sought her out once breakfast was over and Jake had taken Roger into his workshop for an hour or so. She was in the kitchen, putting the newly-washed plates on the big pine dresser that ran along one wall, when Neil cornered her. He closed the door behind him and looked across the room as she anxiously turned to face him.

'The boy seems in quite good form, despite his plaster. Amazing resilience the young have; with us older ones, shock lasts longer, wouldn't you say, Kim?'

'Yes.' Her voice was faint, and she watched him frown. He suddenly strode across to where she stood, and stared at her with stormy eyes.

'And now, suppose you tell me exactly what that ridiculous, self-indulgent trip on to the moor was all about? Good God, you could both have died out there! You're a fool, Kim Hearne.'

His anger was so unexpected that it

took her breath away. Shrinking from him, she could only mutter defensively, 'I'm sorry — I didn't think.' And then, with a surge of resentment at his harshness, she added, 'Maybe it would have been a good thing if I *had* died! I don't have a future, only a past — a filthy, cruel past that just goes on and on haunting me. No one really cares what happens to me, so why should you?'

Roughly, he pulled her to him, his arms an imprisoning circle around her trembling body. 'Because — ' he started to speak, and she suddenly realised he was suffering almost as much as she herself.

But then there was no need to explain, because everything she wanted to know was there, in his kiss.

6

The feeling of Neil's arms around her and the touch of his lips brought back bitter memories to Kim. This was how Bruce had held her and kissed her, and fear and disgust flared up inside her. She couldn't bear letting a man — any man — touch her, let alone kiss her, these days.

Wildly, she struck out at Neil, with one thought only, that she must get away and not fall into the same, fearsome trap again. Bruce had used his kisses to make her forgive and forget, and Neil would probably be the same. But his strength imprisoned her and she was caught within his arms like a creature in a trap, completely at his mercy.

But, Neil's embrace, although strong, was gentle as Bruce's had never been. Against her better judgement, Kim relaxed in his arms and soon found she was returning his kiss.

It had been so long — so very long — since she had last shared such a feeling, for Bruce's kisses had always had strings attached to them. Now his ferocious demands flashed through her mind.

'You're mine, Kim — all mine. Sorry I hurt you just now, I didn't mean it. Come to bed, eh? Give me the little girl I want, darling. Come on, Kim . . . '

She closed her eyes as she relived those terrible moments when she waited for Bruce's hand to punish her procrastination yet again.

'No,' she moaned, trying to get free of the imprisoning arms. 'No, Bruce! No!'

'It's not Bruce, Kim! It's Neil. And I love you.'

Shocked into reality by the low, firm voice that was so utterly different from Bruce's throaty, persuasive whispers, Kim stared into Neil's intent eyes and drew a sobbing breath.

'Neil?' she muttered brokenly. 'Oh, Neil . . . ' And then the tears overflowed as she remembered. Bruce was dead, she had killed him, and this man who held her so carefully, yet with an unbreakable strength, loved her . . .

It was impossible to believe, and yet — Kim's weeping stopped as she searched the face so close to her own and saw the love in Neil's eyes.

He was smiling at her tenderly. 'Cheer up,' he said gently. 'The nightmare's over and this could be the happy ending — if you want it to be.'

He pulled her gently towards him. She felt his thudding heart close to hers, and knew with certainty that his avowal of love was a true one.

Reassured, she laid her head against his chest, savouring his warmth and his strength. When she raised her head again, there was a smile on her lips, and her voice was husky.

'I love you, too, Neil. Oh — so much. But . . . '

'We'll think about the buts later.

Much later. Right now all I want to do is kiss you, and to go on kissing you — '

Kim closed her eyes and felt sheer happiness engulf her. It was a wonderful feeling.

When, eventually, the time came to 'discuss the buts', as Neil had put it, they were walking in the grounds of Badlake House, hands clasped, and a feeling of shared understanding enveloping them both.

Lunch had been eaten and cleared up. Roger was snoozing upstairs in the sumptuous bedroom, Jake was keeping an eye open for possible customers and the late March sunshine, in which they strolled, held a faint promise of early spring.

Kim, warm in her thick sweater and dark corduroy trousers, knew it was time she and Neil cleared up some of the muddles and conflicts that raged around them. For, if they were to abide by the love they had so recently pledged to each other, nothing must remain hidden. And if she suddenly felt nervous at having to face up to her past, she was bravely determined to do her best to succeed.

* * *

Neil paused by the camellia bush, glancing at the countless deep red blooms that glowed like small fires among shiny, dark leaves, before looking back at her.

'Darling, let's talk. No, don't look like that,' he said, as her face paled and her hand in his began to tremble. 'Just remember that I love you, and that nothing is so bad that love can't deal with it. Kim, you must try to realise that I really do mean that.'

Slowly, she nodded. He was right, of course. But talking about Bruce was so painful.

Neil seemed to understand that. He squeezed her fingers. 'OK, so we'll start with Fiona. The girl I happen to be still engaged to.'

Kim watched as his mouth set into grim lines. She pressed his hand encouragingly.

'Tell me,' she said gently.

Neil nodded, and together they walked on down the curving drive, bordered by great, leafy rhododendron bushes. The sun, a pale, distant orb already seeming to regret its spring-like intensity, retreated behind windswept clouds.

'I never loved Fiona, and that's the truth. They say a gentleman never tells — ' Neil's brief smile was twisted as he continued — 'but I can honestly say that she made all the running. And it was easier to go along with it than say no and have to go on looking — '

Abruptly he stopped, turning to look hard at Kim. 'I was looking for a wife,' he explained, straight-faced and serious. 'I wanted someone to love me. I needed a woman in my life — I'd been alone so long. I had this awful void where my family was concerned, and I knew the answer was to fill it with my own, personal family feelings.

'I thought once Fiona and I were married I'd forget about the past, and then, gradually, I knew I'd made the wrong choice. Fiona's a lovely creature. She's charming and she's fun. But inside, well, it's all hardness and ego. Oh, Kim, my darling, she has none of your warmth, of your willingness to share . . . '

They looked at each other with growing perception, and Kim's hand trembled in his. Hesitantly, she sought for words to excuse the woman who had caused her so much pain and renewed terror. 'But — but Fiona isn't all bad, Neil. I mean, she has the guts to say what she feels. And she's brave, willing to fight hard to keep you. I'm not brave at all. I'm — well, a terrible coward, really.'

'Stop it!' Neil's rough words brought a flush of colour to her cheeks and she stared, aghast. But he pulled her close and kissed her forehead, her cheeks, and the soft line of her throat. And she felt in his lips the force of his love for her, and his complete understanding of her.

'You've got a lion's heart, my darling,' he told her softly. 'I've never known anyone as courageous as you. After all — you had the strength to fight Bruce to the death in the end, didn't you?'

Kim shook her head, suddenly unable to meet his gaze. She pulled away and said, 'Let's go on walking. I can't think straight while you're holding me. Neil, I want to tell you about that last night with Bruce. I want to tell you very badly, but — but it's difficult. Please be patient with me.'

He took her hand again. 'Of course I will, love. Take your time, there's no hurry.' He sounded casual, as if she had been talking about something quite unimportant.

Suddenly outraged, Kim swung around to face him, her eyes shadowed by billowing emotions of regret and guilt. 'Oh, but there is, Neil — I *have* to tell you, and as soon as I can, because until I do it's standing between us. I'm not free — I can't be — not completely, until you know about how Bruce died. How I killed him.'

Neil stood, staring. At last he nodded, his hand searching once more for hers. When he found it, Kim sensed a difference in him immediately. His hand was as warm as before, but she knew that he had realised the truth of her words. Suddenly, an invisible barrier had grown between them.

Kim shivered and made a brave attempt to smile and act normally. 'Let's get back, shall we? Roger will be awake and wanting his tea.'

Silently, they retraced their steps to the shadowed, dark house. At the front door Kim impulsively turned round to share a last, intimate moment with Neil — perhaps to convince herself that she had imagined the barrier being there. But Neil was no longer smiling and the hardness in his face had returned.

Jake appeared in the hall as they

entered, his smile banishing some of Kim's dismay. 'Roger is awake, I just took him up a cup of tea. I hope that's OK?'

'Of course, Jake — how kind of you. I'll go up to him now. Neil . . . ' Turning she met his unsmiling gaze and realised with a jolt that he didn't approve of her friendship with Jake.

At any other time the mere idea of such disapproval would have made her laugh — now it only strengthened her uneasy fears about her relationship with Neil. Men were all selfish, jealous, and even violent. Was she wrong in thinking Neil was any different'

He was looking directly at her and she wondered if her thoughts were readable. She said apprehensively, 'I — I'm going up to Roger. I'll be down soon to make some tea for us . . . '

'Don't bother. I'm sure I can master the intricacies of boiling some water.' Neil stalked off to the kitchen with a set face.

Meanwhile, Kim climbed the sweeping

stairs to the bedroom where Roger sat up in the big, curtained bed.

'Jake cut me a sandwich. Look, Mum — cheese, ham and cress. It's super. Would you like a bite?'

Kim sat down on the bed and kissed his forehead. 'No, thanks, love. You finish it — you need building up after that nasty accident.'

'Pooh! It wasn't that bad. And my leg doesn't hurt any more now. Can I get up, Mum?'

'We'll see tomorrow. I'll ring the doctor in the village and ask him to come and look at you.'

'O.K.' Roger wriggled lower down the bed and looked at her wistfully. 'Are we going home soon?'

★ ★ ★

'Home?' The word hit a raw nerve as she thought back to the handsome suburban house where that last terrible row with Bruce had taken place. The house that had been put on the market after his death and which, until she left London two weeks ago, had still been unsold.

'The cottage, silly!' Roger's shrill laugh brought her back to the present. 'Neil said it was our home, remember?'

'Of course I do. Sorry, love, I'd forgotten — '

'Well, I hadn't. I like it there, and I want to go back. It's O.K. here, I s'pose, but — but I was making that rockery, wasn't I? And I liked my bedroom up in the roof. Sort of cosy. This is so big . . . ' He stared around the spacious room disapprovingly, such a tiny mite in the huge bed, and Kim put her arms around him with a surge of love.

He was right, of course — they had a new home and they must return to it. She would tell Neil that it would be better to leave Badlake House. Somehow she and Roger would manage the long walk up and down the drive. And she would feel happier, less threatened, if she wasn't constantly in Neil's company.

What a muddle it all was. Kim stroked Roger's hair pensively. She knew that she loved Neil, and he had said he loved her . . . yet something had already come between them. The memory of Bruce. And her own, paralysing fear.

Sitting there with Roger cuddled against her, Kim was able to relax a little — and in that moment of introspection she realised something else. Her inability to trust Neil completely was forcing him back into his own doubts and conflicts. Everything, it seemed, was her fault . . .

Later that evening, she tried to tell him how she felt as they sat in uneasy silence in the large, draughty drawing-room. She had hoped that Neil would have chosen to light the study fire, but when she had left Roger to join Neil for tea, she found him already settled in the drawing-room. Although they conversed lightly as she poured the tea, the precious moments they had shared earlier were already mere shadows of memory.

Now Kim broke the silence, saying quietly, 'Neil, I'm taking Roger back to the cottage tomorrow.'

He stared across the hearth, his dark eyes unflinching. 'I see.'

'Do you? I don't think so.' She heard her voice grow clipped and hard, but was unable to stop it. 'I need to be away from you, Neil — just for a while. We're too close here.'

'I thought lovers wanted to be close to each other.' Clearly he wasn't trying to understand.

'Of course! But not yet.' Foolishly, she ran out of words and sat there, wondering wretchedly how to explain her problem. His next chilly words caused her to stare at him incredulously.

'It's Jake, I suppose. You're not sure which of us will be best for you. Women are all the same, it seems, always manipulating, doing only what's best for them.'

'No!' The bitterness in his voice made her leave her chair. Going across to kneel beside him, she saw the pain so clearly imprinted on his lean face; he felt as he had when a child — rejected. 'Neil, my darling, it's not Jake. It never could be . . . Only you — I swear it.'

He put a hand on her hair and ran his fingers through her crisp chestnut curls. She watched, holding her breath, as his expression slowly changed to one of resigned acceptance.

'I wish I could believe you . . . '

'But you can!'

'Can I?' Then he made a grab for her, pulling her to him so roughly that her immediate reaction was to shrink back, whimpering, remembering past occasions which had ended in roughness and pain.

'Let me go!' The fatal words hung over them both, as she and Neil stared at each other for a long, wretched moment.

Then releasing her, he stood up and went towards the door, leaving her there by the empty chair, face in her hands, shaking with the fear that she had driven him away for ever.

The door clicked open, and his distant voice said coldly, 'I'm going to the study. To work.'

She heard his footsteps fading down the passage. Stiffly, Kim went back to her chair and sat alone in the silent room, her mind filled with fresh anguish. Whatever she did seemed to be wrong. Whoever she loved failed her. How could she find the strength to go on?

But, later that night as she lay sleepless in the bed beside Roger, the ugly truth finally hit her. It was she who had failed Neil. And, loving him, she accepted that she must be the one to put matters right between them.

She was so occupied with Roger the next morning that she came down late for breakfast. Neil had cooked his own and was on his way out of the kitchen. She felt torn apart — for she loved him and yearned for him to be near her — yet she longed also for him to return to London and give her the breathing space she so badly needed.

As if he read her thoughts, Neil said, in his old, impersonal manner, 'I'm staying on for a few days. Trying to get to grips with this damned biography I've started.' Suddenly, his dark eyes caught hers. 'Oh, don't worry,' he added coldly. 'I'll shut myself away in the study. You can forget me.'

Watching him stride down the hall, Kim realised the last words had contained a double meaning and she caught her breath as the pain seared through her.

It was an enormous relief to get busy, organising their return to the cottage, and again she was grateful for Jake's unobtrusive help.

'We'll all drive down in the Capri,' he suggested, 'then I'll go on to do whatever shopping you need. Mr Leston said it was all right for me to give you a hand.'

Kim decided to ignore the last

sentence, and so, by the middle of the morning she and an elated Roger were happily reinstated in Badlake Cottage. Roger sat on the hearth-rug by the fire drawing, while Kim brought in logs and prepared a list of groceries for Jake.

The shabby homeliness of the cottage, after the elegant spaciousness of the big house, was reassuring, and Kim's spirits slowly began to rise. Roger was a demanding patient, and it was easy to keep her mind occupied by entertaining, and restraining him.

Jake asked, with his usual shy smile, if he might come down for coffee during the evening. The craft show was drawing near and he wanted her advice on a couple of matters.

'Of course, Jake. Please come — we'll be glad to see you,' Kim said, returning his smile unthinkingly. She needed his support and undemanding friendship, which she could repay by helping him organise the craft stall. Surely, even Neil would see nothing wrong in that.

But it was Mary Carew, with her

189

forthright honesty, who put the matter into blunt perspective the following day. She came to inquire about Roger, and shared a cup of coffee by the crackling fire.

Following Kim into the kitchen, as she went to refill the mugs, Mary said quietly, 'You're the subject of village gossip, I'm afraid, my dear. You and that Jake McKenzie. The shop was full of it, they're practically laying bets on when the wedding will be . . . '

Kim gasped, nearly dropping the mug she was filling. Deftly, Mary recovered it. 'All your own fault, you know. You and Neil have been fighting, from what I can gather. You've hurt him very badly, and now you're amusing yourself with poor old Jake. It's not on, Kim — you're behaving like an unthinking teenager. I'd expected better of you than this.'

Angrily, Kim realised the truth of Mary's accusation, but couldn't bring herself to acknowledge her own guilt. 'How dare you! What a rotten thing to say. And I thought we were friends!'

'We are. That's why I said what I did. Look, my dear . . . ' Mary's arm was around Kim's stiff shoulders, her bright eyes full of understanding sympathy. 'We all have hard lessons to learn in life, and one of the most important is to avoid bringing pain to other people through our own, unthinking selfishness. Now, Jake's a lonely man, and you're encouraging him to fall for you. That's hard on him — and doesn't have a future, because you love Neil, don't you?'

'And what if I do? It's no business of yours. Oh, I wish I'd never come down here! Everything's gone wrong since I came . . . ' Kim stared furiously into Mary's face and then turned away, petulantly shrugging out of Mary's embrace. 'Do you want this coffee or not?'

'No, thanks.' Mary's voice was level and she still smiled.

Kim felt a pang of regret; half of her wanted Mary to flare up so that they could have a really good row, but how could she deal with someone who kept her temper and still acted as a friend?

Kim followed Mary back into the room where Roger was. He looked up from the table, where he was making a Lego model, and his face was creased with frown lines. 'Why were you shouting, Mum?' he asked.

Kim sat down and put her arms about him, ashamed of herself. Mary's words had struck home.

'Sorry, love. I forgot what a loud voice I've got! What're you making? Oh, yes, I see — a cottage. Very good! Don't forget to put a chimney on.'

She looked up to see Mary disappearing out of the front door and heard the bright voice say unaffectedly, 'Cheerio! See you both again soon.' Then the Land-Rover roared into life and drove away. Kim felt lonely all of a sudden and deeply ashamed of herself. She didn't deserve to have a friend like Mary Carew.

In the evening, once Roger was

safely asleep and the darkness outside made her huddle by the glowing fire, Kim reviewed the morning's unpleasant scene and knew what she had to do. When, as was the custom each evening, Jake appeared at the door, she asked him to look after Roger while she went down to the phone box. Mary was in and Kim tried her best to apologise, but it wasn't easy.

'I — I was ridiculous this morning, Mary. Please forgive me . . . can you?'

Kim held her breath, waiting to be told off again, for she knew by now what a blunt character Mary Carew was.

But her apology was accepted, and Mary's voice was as warm and serene as ever, as she said airily, 'Don't think twice about it, my dear — except that I hope you'll consider the sermon I preached at you! I know about life, I learned the hard way, just like you're doing. Now, let's forget it all.

'Look, what about letting Roger come up and see me one day? If he'd care to he could stay for a night or two. The bay mare is about to foal and he'd probably find that interesting . . . and Number Three could come with him.'

Humbly, Kim replied, 'That's marvellous of you, Mary. I know he'd love to come. And — and thanks.'

'All right, Kim. I'll be over to fetch the lad tomorrow when I do the weekly shopping . . . about ten o'clock. Good night, my dear. Sleep well.'

And for once, Kim did sleep well; no nightmares forcing her to wake with wretched memories and a pounding heart. When she awoke next morning the day was balmy, and her mood matched it. She felt a new strength had been pumped into her while she slept, and that somehow she would find a way of coming to terms with problems that still dogged her.

Soon after breakfast, there was a knock at the door and Dr Porter, whose day it was to visit the village Health Centre, smiled down at her as he stooped to avoid the low beam of the door.

'Neil Leston rang and asked me to have a look at your lad, Mrs Hearne — said you wondered how long he'd need to keep the plaster on.'

'Oh! Please come in, Doctor . . . ' Kim was moved by Neil's thoughtfulness, and watched as Roger's leg was carefully inspected.

'It's improving well, Mrs Hearne. Another week, I'd say, and then I'll fix an appointment at the hospital to have it off.'

'My leg?' Roger squealed.

'No, lad, just the plaster!' The old doctor chuckled.

'But — not for a *week*?' Roger's crestfallen expression made both Kim and the friendly doctor smile.

'Only another seven days, son — and you're going to stay with Mrs Carew today. You'll be so busy you'll forget the old plaster.'

Once Dr Porter had gone, Kim and Roger began packing an overnight bag.

Before they were finished, Mary arrived and sat by the fire with Number Three, safely contained in a cat box, on her knee.

'Have you thought about what I said yesterday?' Mary asked bluntly, when Roger rushed outside to collect some important toy.

Kim looked at her, flushing, as she answered, after some slight hesitation, 'Yes, I have. You — you certainly pull a hard punch, Mary.'

'So I've often been told.' The lovely, ageing face held a sardonic smile, but there was warmth in Mary's bright eyes.

'Well, it hit home all right.'

'Good. I'm so glad you've finally seen the error of your ways, my dear.' Mary stood up, the cat box firmly clutched in her hands, with Number Three wailing unhappily inside it. She put her face down to the box, saying softly. 'All right, little one, it's only a ten minute drive and then you'll be out of it. Hang on. Now, look Kim . . . '

Again, her eyes found Kim's. 'One more thing to say. Want to hear it?'

Kim shrugged grudgingly. 'Go on, then.'

'Er — Roger, can you carry Number Three out to the Land-Rover? Very carefully, mind. Don't fall over your silly old plaster or you'll upset the poor creature even more.

'Well, Kim . . . ' Mary waited till the boy was outside again. 'Your problems won't go till you learn to let people into your life on *their* terms, not simply on yours. OK, that's all!' She grinned. 'Now I'm off — and don't worry, my dear, I'll look after the little lad as if he were my own. Just wish he were, actually . . . '

* * *

Once the Land-Rover had driven away, with smiles and farewell shouts from both Mary and Roger, the cottage seemed depressingly quiet. However, as Kim prepared a hasty snack, prior to walking up to Badlake House to resume her neglected duties there, she began to realise that true friendship was a wonderful and rare gift.

It had taken courage for Mary to tell her those blunt home-truths, and gradually she understood that she must take a fresh look at her life and her relationships, as Mary had suggested.

Jake must be painlessly, but firmly discouraged — and Neil? Her heart turned over. Somehow she had to prove to Neil that she needed and loved him — and understood his difficulties. But it wasn't going to be easy.

Not until four o'clock did Kim see anything of Neil, but wherever she was in the house, polishing the antiques or studying her reference books in the library, the halting sound of his typewriter was a constant interruption to her restless thoughts. Clearly, the machine was either old and broken, or Neil was a very poor typist . . .

Kim carried the tea tray down to the study, balancing it cautiously as she knocked on the door. 'Tea-time!' she called, and was relieved to hear the lightness in her own voice.

Suddenly the machine was silent. Neil's chair scraped back on the waxed floorboards, and then he stood at the door, his face carefully non-committal, but a certain unexpected warmth was plain to see in his dark, brooding eyes.

'What excellent timing! I was just thinking about tea.'

Kim fought the impulse to put down the tray and fly into his arms. Instead, she smiled casually.

'How's it going? I've heard you working away for hours on end.' She put the tray on the littered table.

Neil swept some books from the chair beside the fire, opposite his own. Wryly he said, 'Well, the ideas are there — and the words, too. It's that damned machine that lets me down.'

'You sound like the traditional workman, blaming his tools.' She lowered her eyes. Things were going well between them so far, but she sensed she must keep a grip on her surging feelings, and not spoil their new rapport.

'Mmm, I suppose I do. I think I'll take my draft back to town tomorrow, and let Miss Gordon at the office whizz it off on her miraculous word processor.' His voice lightened. 'This cake's excellent, did you make it?'

Taken by surprise, Kim felt herself colour foolishly. If only this new, friendly relationship could go on for ever.

'Actually, I did,' she confessed. 'Walnut and honey.'

'Another piece, please.' He was watching her with a smile in his eyes, and Kim realised he was being as cautious as she was. Her heart did a little somersault at the thought. She no longer wanted him to leave Badlake House, not now that things were improving between them. Suddenly a brilliant idea dawned on her.

'I'll type your book for you! I worked

200

as a secretary for several years before — before I married.'

'Will you really? That's wonderful. But on that ghastly old machine?'

'I'm sure I can manage.'

Kim watched Neil stretching his long legs in front of him, while leaning back in his chair. He smiled thoughtfully. 'Then I don't have to go chasing back to town, after all.' He shot her a quick, appraising glance. 'Funny, but for the first time in years I'm enjoying being here at Badlake.'

'I'm glad.'

'And so am I.'

They looked at each other with growing awareness until he broke the silence by saying, with a note of surprise in his voice, 'You know, this isn't a bad little room. Small, but comfortable. And in spite of all those long faces!' Half-humorously he nodded at the sepia photographs covering the walls. 'I've felt very much at home today. I mean — '

Suddenly his face grew serious. 'I

mean, at home in the truest sense of the word; relaxed and comfortable. Even happy, I think. Now, isn't that strange?'

'No,' Kim said firmly. 'This is your home. And this is your family, watching you write about them and sorting out their photos. What could be more natural or happier than that? Oh, Neil — ' Abruptly, she leaned forward in her chair and stared at him with a pleading smile.

'I do hope it's all helping you. I mean, making you realise that . . . '

Confused, she shook her head. It had been right for Mary Carew to preach, but how could she say such things to Neil? He would think she was interfering in matters which didn't concern her. He wouldn't understand that his happiness was important to her.

But it seemed that he did. 'Go on,' he said drily, and his quiet voice held a note of encouragement. 'Go on, Kim. Please.'

'Well . . . ' She sank back into her chair and anxiously sought the right words. 'It's *you* who has pushed away your family — not the other way around, really. It's *your* fault you feel so badly about them. After all, we can all choose how we feel about things, and you've made the wrong choice . . . and, as a result, you're ruining your life, Neil.'

Then Kim stopped, terrified that she'd said too much. Apprehensively, she watched his face. Abruptly, he got up and went to the window; his usual move when he needed to control his anger.

* * *

When eventually he spoke, his voice was subdued, and it was with great relief that she heard him say from behind her, 'Thank you. That was long over-due, I suppose. And you're right, of course. I've been building up my distrust and dislike of families and close relationships ever since I was a child. I can see it now. But . . . '

Neil was close to her, his hands on her tense shoulders, and his voice so low it only just reached her. 'But I've still got some way to go before I can start afresh. Help me, my darling — will you?'

'Of course I will! Oh, Neil, Neil . . . ' She was on her feet, going into his arms with happy abandon and discovering, as they kissed, that she was no longer afraid of his strength and possession.

'Thank God I found you, Kim.'

'But that's just what I feel about you! Hold me tightly, love, I still can't really believe it . . . '

For a few, precious moments the world was bright again, fears dissolving and hope born anew. And then the telephone rang and Neil's dark eyebrows winged up in exasperation. 'Let it ring, eh?'

Kim reluctantly disengaged herself and smiled back at him as she leaned over the table to pick up the receiver.

'It might just be Mary. She's got Roger staying with her for a couple of nights. Hello? Oh . . . '

'Is that you, Mrs — er — Hearne?'

It was Fiona. Abruptly, Kim's over-flowing happiness died. She glanced up and saw Neil's expression now matched her own.

He grabbed at the phone. 'Here, I'll deal with her . . . '

'No.' Kim knew she must handle Fiona herself, for despite the charm in that honeyed voice, Kim instinctively knew she meant fresh trouble. 'Yes, Fiona, Kim here,' she said quietly. 'What do you want?' She held the receiver an inch away from her ear so that Neil could hear the conversation.

'That doesn't sound very friendly!' Fiona bantered. 'What do I want, indeed! My dear girl, you know damn well just what I want — Neil, and no other. And I mean to get him, too. Now, look here, I'm coming down tomorrow to see him — and you. We've got to have it all out.'

Fiona's voice grew hard. 'And as for you — well, you'd better start packing your bags. Somehow I don't think you'll want to stay on in sunny Devon much longer!'

Kim heard a click as Fiona put down the phone and then the dialling tone returned. Shaking, she replaced the receiver and turned to Neil to find him watching her, frowning angrily.

'What on earth was all that about? My God, she'd better not start getting up to her old tricks again. It's all right, my darling, she can't hurt us any more. Kim, I promise I won't let anything hurt you ever again . . . '

But he was too close, his arms were once again like Bruce's, catching her, holding her against her will. Something flipped in Kim's overwrought mind. The voices in her imagination grew confused. Over Neil's words Bruce's husky voice became ugly reality. This had all happened before, she told herself wildly — she knew this scene by heart.

What had Bruce said, on that last, ghastly night, as he pulled her into his arms after a terrible row, leering down at her as she trembled in his unwanted embrace?

'Kim, I know I've been up to a few tricks in the past, but it's all right, darling. I promise, Kim, I won't hurt you ever again. But right now I want you, and I'm going to have you — '

Kim spun away, out of Neil's arms, insanely certain that he was simply trying to soften her up in order to get his own way with her, just as Bruce had done.

Stepping backwards, she let her hands flicker over the littered table. She was looking for something, looking for the dreadful weapon which she had used on Bruce. But it wasn't there any longer, so she flew out of the room. Sobbing as she ran down the cold, dark-shadowed drive, she headed for the cottage where at least she could be alone to think what she must do next.

7

Kim ran wildly down the long, winding drive. Dusk was falling fast, and in its wake a wind had blown up, shaking the trees and bushes as it funnelled relentlessly through the encircling grounds of Badlake House.

Her nerves even more jangled by the rustling of the branches and leaves, Kim almost fell into Jake's startled arms, as she careered round a corner.

'Kim! What's wrong? You look terrible . . . '

She stared blindly at his alarmed face, her voice shrill and overwrought as she finally blurted out, 'I can't stay here any longer. I've got to get away Fiona's told everyone what I did. Oh, let me go, Jake, let me go!'

But he held her firmly, slowly bringing her back to her senses as he said sharply, 'You're not going anywhere. Not until you've got all this off your chest. Let's go back to the cottage and have a talk. Yes, Kim, I mean it — you're in need of help, and I wouldn't call myself your friend if I let you go off alone like this.'

In the cottage he lit the fire and made tea, while Kim sat down, trying to get warm and control her nerves. The tea helped, and so did Jake's straightforward questions.

'So — tell me what all this is about. I knew there was something on your mind the very first day we met. What is it, Kim?'

Miserably, she stared across the hearth, digging her nails into her tense palms as reluctantly, in a whisper, she told him the truth. 'I — I killed my husband . . . '

Jake drew back, sucking in his breath. 'My God!' he said in a barely-audible whisper.

Bitterly, Kim asked, 'I've shocked you, haven't I?'

'Well to be honest, yes — just a

bit.' Now it was Jake's turn to hesitate before going on lamely. 'I thought — I thought maybe you'd been jilted; come down here to get away — that sort of thing.'

Kim gave a cold, mirthless laugh. 'I came here to try to escape from the rest of the world. Particularly the newspapers. They had a heyday while the court case was on.

Leaning forward, she suddenly felt it imperative to tell him more and get the horror out of her mind. 'It wasn't murder, Jake — the verdict was manslaughter. The judge said I'd had such a terrible time with Bruce — mitigating circumstances, he called it — so I was free to go.

'Oh, I had to keep in touch with my probation officer, that sort of thing, but he said that he trusted me. It was the newspapers that kept up the hunt, you see.'

'You poor kid. I can imagine.' Jake's gentle smile was sympathetic, and Kim felt some of her anxiety subside. 'But you said just now that Fiona — Miss Cartwright — had told everyone. What did you mean?'

Kim sighed wretchedly. 'She told the Press. And that means everyone in the village now knows who I really am and what I did.' Her anguish returned as she hid her face in her hands, adding in a trembling voice, 'I can't take any more, Jake. I just can't.'

'But you said you got off, so what are you afraid of? I don't know the details of the case, of course, but it sounds as if your old man deserved all he got. Come on, Kim, buck up — it's not as if you'd been sent to prison, now is it?'

Gradually she forced herself to meet his eyes and consider what he'd just said. 'No,' she admitted. 'But it's the shame — the terrible shame of having killed him . . . Telling the police I did it, and how it happened. Being in court, with everyone looking at me. Hearing that awful word, *murder* . . . '

For a long moment there was silence,

as once again she fought for self-control.

Then Jake spoke, in a quiet, hesitant voice. 'I know how you feel, Kim.'

Their eyes met and she saw pain cloud his face. Suddenly she understood.

'You mean, *you've* been in prison? Because you did something like I did.'

Jake held her gaze. 'I hurt someone — a woman. It was grievous bodily harm. She let me down, and I couldn't handle the situation. I went berserk . . .'

Kim watched, fascinated, as his right hand formed into a fist. 'I didn't kill her — but I did hurt her badly. I did six months for it.'

Kim could see it all now. Woman-hater — the name the unthinking village had given Jake was an apt one. Yet she had thought he was growing fond of her . . .

As if reading her mind, he said in a low voice, 'I couldn't trust anyone after that — especially any woman. And then you came here, and it was different.' He looked at her with his direct, penetrating gaze, and a hint of a smile appeared on his lips. 'You've done a lot for me, Kim, and I thank you for it.'

The colour rushed to her pale cheeks. 'But . . .'

Unexpectedly, he grinned broadly and sat back. 'Oh, I don't mean I fell for you, but you've made me realise that women aren't all the same. My life's happier these days. I'm able to cope better . . .'

Smiling back at him, Kim said shyly, 'I'm glad if I helped, Jake. But . . .'

'No buts. You've been a good friend, and I'd like to repay what you've done. So I'm going to give you a bit of advice — if you'll take it, that is.'

More advice? Kim's smiled faded. First Mary Carew, and now Jake. But she recalled how Mary's hard-hitting words had helped, and so, resignedly, she nodded at Jake.

'OK, let's have it.'

'Well, it seems to me you've got

to stop panicking about the world knowing who you are, and what you did. Most people are far too concerned with their own worries to care about others — even murderers.'

Kim winced. 'It wasn't — '

Sharply, Jake cut off her excuse. 'Of course it was. Murder, manslaughter — all the same. Only a technical difference, isn't it? But, under the circumstances it sounds as if any woman worth her salt would've done what you did. What did Mr Leston say when you told him?'

Kim shrank back in her seat. 'I didn't. I mean, not at first. And then, when Fiona told him, I tried to leave . . . '

Jake stared sternly at her. 'You've got to face up to what you've done, Kim. Running away is no use. Surely Mr Leston thinks that way, doesn't he?'

'Yes . . . ' Again Kim's thoughts returned to that dreadful last scene with Bruce.

Jake's next words echoed her thoughts.

'You've got to stop letting it haunt you like this, Kim. Look at it rationally; tell yourself it happened, you did the only thing possible and now it's over. Then you can start living again. I tell you, I *know*.'

As she stared, he rose and came to her side, his smile suddenly warm and strong. He patted her clasped hands clumsily.

'Believe me, you'll feel better once it's out of your mind. Share it all with Neil Leston.' He paused, his gaze sharpening. 'He loves you, doesn't he?'

Dumbly, she nodded, seeing a brief flash of anguish in Jake's knowing eyes. Then his smile returned.

'He's a lucky guy. Don't let him down, Kim.' And then, once again, Jake's expression was back to its normal shy anonymity. 'Well, if you're OK, I'll be on my way.'

Kim followed him to the door. 'Jake, thanks for everything,' she said unevenly. 'You've made me feel so much better.'

'That's what friends are for. Right?'

Her acknowledging smile followed him into the darkness, as he left the cottage, heading back to Badlake House, leaving her alone, but with a marvellous new strength glowing inside her chilled body.

★ ★

Early next morning, as she left the cottage to begin the long walk up the drive, her new-found strength was abruptly tested.

A car crunched to a halt by her side, and as she looked towards the driver her heart fell heavily, like a plummeting stone. She knew that face too well — the straggly little moustache and the spaced-out, discoloured teeth that gave such a rat-like look to the man staring back at her.

'Well, well! So this is where you're hiding, eh? I told you I'd find you in the end!' The voice was loud, sharp and rich with self-satisfaction.

Kim forced herself to stand her ground as Jake's advice filtered through her mind. She looked at the reporter who had previously hounded her every moment so relentlessly.

'I think I can guess how you found me, but I'd like to know for certain.'

An unpleasant smile puckered the man's face. 'Someone in London pulled a few strings. Fiona Cartwright, the bird who's engaged to the chap living here at Badlake House, told her cousin, who's editor of the *Daily Clarion*, that she'd met you here. And the story got around. I mean, you were hot news, my girl! Even down here in this godforsaken place.'

His smile faded and he added glumly, 'I had the bad luck to be sent down here a couple of weeks ago, but I managed to pick up the message . . . '

He stroked his untidy moustache with nicotine-stained fingers, enjoying her discomfort as he stared at her through the car window. 'Everyone knows,' he warned her. 'Your name, where you live, and — ' leaning towards her, he lowered his voice dramatically ' — and what you did — how you killed your old man!'

Then, as he realised Kim was simply staring back at him, not showing a trace of emotion, he added, with a note of disappointment, 'Suppose I'd better be on my way. I'm going to interview someone about a craft show — Jake McKenzie. Do you know him? Got a flat here, hasn't he?'

Kim pulled herself together. 'You've been so clever in finding me,' she said icily, 'I'm sure you don't need any help in tracing someone with a proper address.' And she walked away, leaving the reporter frowning after her.

It was good to feel that she'd had the last word. Kim clenched her teeth and tried to forget the unpleasant little episode. But as soon as Badlake House came into view and she saw Fiona's car parked by the front porch, her anxiety came hurtling back.

Now there would be more unpleasantness, and more heart-searching. Just for a moment she wanted to turn and run, but she remembered Jake's advice — running would get her nowhere.

Taking a deep breath, she entered the house, grimly going in search of Fiona Cartwright. It wasn't hard to find her; the cultured voice was ringing through the house, all charm gone, a note of desperation audible in its shrillness.

'What do you mean, it's all off?' Fiona screamed, as Kim knocked timidly at the half-open drawing-room door.

'For Heaven's sake, Fiona, calm down and let's discuss this sensibly.' Suddenly Neil was at the door, his dark eyes warming at Kim's appearance and a quick smile relieving the grimness of his expression. 'Come in,' he said, taking her by the hand. 'I'm glad you're here. Fiona's having hysterics, I'm afraid.'

Kim smiled nervously and stayed

by the door as Neil shut it behind her before returning to face Fiona, who stood by the fireplace looking unfamiliarly distraught and untidy. Her usual lovely halo of hair was dishevelled and her smart business suit creased, as if she'd slept in it. She glared ferociously at Kim.

'I like that — hysterics, indeed! *She's* the one you ought to be pacifying, not me, Neil. *She's* a killer, and there's no knowing when she'll attack you!'

'Stop it!' Neil's palm slapped Fiona's cheek with a resounding whack and she stood open-mouthed, shocked into silence, fingering the livid weal on her face.

The atmosphere could have been cut with a knife. Kim was the first to break the silence, her hand on Neil's arm. 'You shouldn't have done that,' she said in a low voice. 'Violence is never the answer, Neil — '

As if released from her dramatic pose, Fiona swung round, glaring at Kim. 'How right you are, Kim Hearne!'

she exulted, her voice ringing through the silence. 'And you should know — look where violence got you! Into a court room, and now you're on the run, going from place to place, looking for somewhere to hide, someone to take you in. Well, let me tell you this — *no one's* going to help, because no one wants you!'

Her grating words came to a sharp halt. Kim took an involuntary step back, daunted by the look of hatred and enjoyment on Fiona's contorted face. She was once again at the end of her tether, and she had a sickening feeling that Fiona's words were true. Perhaps after all there was only one solution for her — to run, and go on running, for the rest of her life.

Then Neil's arm was around her, strong and possessive, his voice emphatic in her car as he said, '*I* want you, Kim, and I always will. Don't let this insane woman upset you any more. You're safe with me, safe for ever, Kim.'

She had no words and no strength

left to do anything but bury her head against his shoulder. She knew he loved her, but this declaration of his fidelity and support was almost too much for her. Silently, she rested in his arms, waiting for the storm of Fiona's wrath to subside.

The end came quickly. 'I don't believe it,' Fiona said slowly, with almost childish simplicity. 'I just don't believe you, Neil! You can't feel like that about a — killer!'

Neil's arm tightened protectively around Kim's body. 'Labels don't mean anything to me, Fiona,' he said quietly. 'Not any more. Kim is a woman — just as you are — and I love her.'

'But you said you loved me!' Once again, Fiona's voice was shrill and harsh.

Neil nodded. 'I thought I did,' he confessed. 'But I made a big mistake.' He paused for a moment. 'Fiona, we all make mistakes. Kim was mistaken when she married a man who drove her to self-protective violence. Luckily, you and I have found out we don't really belong together in good time — '

'You mean you're leaving me?'

With a note of near-fondness in his voice, Neil said simply, 'We were never really together, my dear.'

Kim raised her head as the tears on her cheeks dried, and her heart slowed down from its panic-stricken tattoo to a regular beat. She looked at Neil's calm face and saw him smiling at her. A great surge of gratitude and thankfulness swept through her and she was able to turn and face the woman staring at her with such disbelieving eyes.

'I'm sorry, Fiona. Really sorry.'

Her words died away, and at last the room seemed to be relieved of all tension. In the fireplace, a log slipped sideways, and Neil went to poke it back into place. In the distance the front door bell rang, and normal life seemed to resume.

Bitterly, Fiona said, 'You two deserve each other. I just hope you'll be happy, although I doubt it.' As she turned to look at her reflection in the mirror above the mantelpiece, patting her hair and smoothing down her creased skirt, she added, 'Actually, I'm quite glad to be out of all this — it's been so sordid. Murder, violence, everlasting rows, and this ghastly old ruin of a house. I'll be much better off back in town.'

A knock at the door interrupted her flippant remarks. Jake's head appeared. 'A customer,' he said shortly, 'in the library.'

Kim went out of the room without a backward glance. Somewhere inside her a new courage was born. It was easy now to leave Fiona for Neil to deal with, knowing that her words no longer had the power to wound.

Kim went to meet the pair of French tourists, already examining a fine mahogany bookcase, self-assured and confident. This was her job and she was beginning to accept that she was good at it.

★ ★ ★

It was mid-morning before the sale was amicably completed, and Neil joined her in the porch as Monsieur and Madame Benoit drove away with friendly smiles and waves.

He drew her towards him, looking searchingly into her eyes. 'You're an amazing woman, darling. I eavesdropped for the last few minutes. You organised them beautifully, down to the crating arrangements of the furniture and the business with the credit card. I have a feeling that you and I are going to make a huge success of Badlake Antiques.'

Lovingly, Kim relaxed in his arms. 'I enjoy it,' she admitted. 'And I'm learning so much.' Suddenly memories of Fiona flew back. Kim's face clouded. 'Where's Fiona?'

'Gone,' Neil said tersely. 'Her grand exit was spoiled, so she got out as fast as possible. I don't think we'll see her again.'

'Thank goodness. Though I'm sorry for her — she loved you, Neil. She must be very unhappy . . . '

'She'll recover.' Neil's tone was dry, with a hint of amusement. 'Fiona's not the sort to die of a broken heart. Darling . . . ' He paused, and Kim saw a look of determination settle on his face.

'What is it?' A slight feeling of uneasiness nagged at her mind but she pushed it aside. Everything was working out, and there was no need to worry any more. Neil was here, supporting and trusting her. She could rely on whatever he asked of her.

But his next words sent the colour from her cheeks, making her draw back from his embrace. 'I want us to go to the craft show this afternoon, love,' he said gently, his eyes never leaving her drawn face.

'But — but . . . ' She struggled in his arms, to no avail, as they remained rock-firm about her. 'I can't, Neil! Everyone will stare. They know who

226

I am now. You can't possibly ask me to go — it's unfair of you. How could you ask such a thing?'

'Because I love you.' His smile had gone, replaced by a firmness that dismayed her even further. She knew by now that when he'd made up his mind nothing would change it. 'Because I want you to realise it's all over — all behind you.'

'It's not! It'll never be over!' Now the old panic had returned, and she was hitting out at him, incapable once again of doing anything other than fight those agonising memories.

Neil held her, unprotesting as her fists pounded on his chest and shoulders.

'Oh, God,' Kim whimpered, hiding her face. 'What am I doing? I'm so sorry, Neil, I didn't mean to hurt you, I love you. You know I love you . . . '

'It's all right, my darling. I understand.' Suddenly a suggestion of laughter crept into his voice. 'You're stronger than you look,' he said.

Gently, his hand cupped her chin

and he looked into her frightened eyes. 'Look,' he told her, tenderly, 'you're not alone anymore. I'm with you — whatever you do, wherever you go.

'And I'll be there this afternoon, if they stare and remember seeing your face in the papers. They'll probably look and whisper for a minute or so, and then they'll think of something else, and you'll be forgotten. We'll be together, my love, and the ordeal will be over. Done with, once and for all.'

Trembling, Kim nodded her assent, but could find no answer, because Neil's mouth came swiftly down to silence her stumbling words.

★ ★ ★

Amazingly, it was just as he had described, Kim discovered, as the afternoon slid past. The craft show took place in and around an ancient stone barn which stood on the village green, close to the church. As the clock struck halfpast two, the great oak doors opened, and a stream of waiting villagers — Neil and Kim amongst them — filed in to wander around and look at the various stalls.

It was a relief to get out of the blustering April weather. Kim nervously followed Neil, with her hand in his, as he led her to one stall after another, paying no attention to the occasional curious glances and murmurs of, 'Afternoon, Mr Leston.'

'Look at these, corn dollies. How about this one, to keep the witches away from our home?' Neil held up a decorative creation of twisted straw and Kim nodded, bemused.

'It's pretty,' she agreed.

Neil's hand tightened on hers. 'Ah, but look — here's real beauty for you. Local silver-smithing, done in the next village. Aren't they great?'

Staring down at rows of well-presented delicate silver jewellery, Kim suddenly felt that she was being watched. Raising her eyes, she met those of the stall-holder, a middle-aged man with unkempt hair and shabby clothes. His frown seared through her.

'You're Kim Hearne, aren't you?' The harsh words rang out above the chattering voices, and an unexpected silence descended. Kim fought back the urge to scream and break it, as Neil kept hold of her hand.

She took a deep breath and forced herself to stare back at the contemptuous gaze of the silversmith.

'Yes, I am.' Her quiet voice evoked a buzz of excitement around the big barn.

The man muttered unpleasantly. 'You've got a nerve — coming here.'

Icily, Neil interrupted, 'She has as much right here as you have.' He pulled her by the hand. 'Come on, Kim — let's move on.' And, without giving her time to answer, he added quietly, as subdued gossip followed them to the next stall, 'I was going to buy you something, but I think we'll wait and find a more congenial salesman, shall we?'

Somehow Kim managed to smile. She squeezed his fingers. 'Thanks, Neil — you're marvellous. I — I couldn't do this without you.'

'And you don't have to, my love. Keep your chin up, we're halfway there.'

They inspected the local pottery stall and Kim, almost afraid to look up, was amazed to have a small, beautifully-crafted stoneware jug pushed into her hand by the woman behind the laden trestle counter.

'I'd like you to have this,' she whispered with a warm smile. 'You've got guts — and I admire that. Don't let that old crosspatch Benbow get you down, he puts all his love into his silver, and he hasn't got any left over for people! Good luck, Mrs Hearne . . . '

Kim's head was held a little higher as she gratefully accepted the mug and the comforting reassurance. She looked at Neil, as they moved on to look at a spectacular display of dried flowers and sculptures of bleached driftwood.

'You were right,' she murmured reluctantly, 'they've seen me now, and the ghastly moment's over. And not everyone thinks so badly of me, after all . . . '

Neil's strong arm hugged her close. 'I told you,' he said simply. 'Now — let's go and fight our way through the crush around the coffee bar . . . '

Again, heads turned round and voices fell and then rose in busy whispers as he bought two coffees. Kim recognised the woman from the Post Office, their eyes meeting with a clash. Just as she was holding her breath, ready for a grim accusation or it deliberate snub, the woman looked away, suddenly gripping the arm of a nearby acquaintance.

Her voice had an excited ring to it, which reached Kim and Neil as they drank their coffee at the side of the little bar.

'Have you heard?' Gladys Beer demanded. 'It was in the local paper today — mind you, I wasn't too surprised.'

Her companion seemed bemused. 'What are you talking about, Glad?'

The beady eyes gleamed. 'Why, that Harry Grainger! Came off at the first fence in the second race — broke his arm, the paper said. His old mum'll be in despair. Never seems to stay on a horse for more than five minutes at a time, does he? I always said he was too wispy to be a jockey. Thin little boy he was, as I remember . . . '

Kim met Neil's amused smile, and was suddenly able to return it. Straightening her shoulders, she replaced the empty cup on the bar and slipped her arm into the crook of his.

'OK, you win. I've had my bad time, and thank goodness I'm now forgotten. Sounds as if young Harry is the man of the moment now . . . '

'He's a local lad who turned professional,' Neil explained, 'and I'm afraid his accident-proneness is much more interesting to the inhabitants of

Badlake than your previous London goings-on . . . '

His smile faded and he drew her close to him, regardless of the passing crowds and occasional amused glances. 'You've done well, my darling, and I'm proud of you. But now, well, I — I — '

Kim had never known him at a loss for words. She searched his face. 'What is it?'

'Just an idea.' He seemed almost apologetic.

'Tell me. Look, over there, where it's quiet — we can sit down for a minute behind the leather stall.'

Halfway across to the stall, they were suddenly confronted by a small, fierce bundle of energy who grinned into their startled faces as he trundled along in his clumsy plaster case.

'Mum! Neil!' Roger shouted exuberantly. 'Hello! It's me!'

★ ★ ★

234

'Darling!' Kim bent to hug his strong little body, feeling a glow of happiness, as she returned Roger's affectionate kisses.

Then he fought to get away, staring wide-eyed at her. 'I don't have to come home yet, do I? The foal should arrive tonight, and I've got to be there. Auntie Mary said she couldn't do without me . . .'

From behind Kim's shoulder, a familiar voice said warmly, 'I do so appreciate having a man around the house. Can you spare him another day or two, my dear?'

Kim met Mary's bright gaze and nodded happily. 'Of course. If you're sure he's no trouble?'

'I'm not a trouble, honest I'm not. I'm being really good!' Roger's self-important voice made them all laugh.

Neil playfully ruffled his hair. 'You've got your plaster filthy, young man. It's time it came off, surely? I'll have to bring my electric saw along.'

'Tuesday, the doctor said. Electric

235

saw? Really and truly?' Roger's eyes twinkled with a mixture of mirth and mock alarm. 'Come on, Auntie Mary, you said we could go and see Jake's models. Bye, Mum. Bye, Neil!'

Mary Carew obediently followed the boy, looking back over her shoulder with a smile. 'Sorry, but you see how things are!'

Kim's smile followed her ebullient son as he gamely hobbled across to the stall where Jake stood, smiling a welcome.

She glanced at Neil apologetically. 'He's always liked his own way, I'm afraid.'

'He's a great boy,' Neil assured her. 'I think we'll get along fine when we all settle down together.'

'Settle . . . ?' Kim seized on the word and searched his face for the meaning of the unexpected phrase.

Neil drew her into a shadowy corner where two folding chairs faced each other in solitude, quite forgotten by the passing crowds.

'Yes, settle,' he said quietly, but with great firmness. 'You, me, and Roger. Oh, and that damned cat, of course. All of us together, in a house which you shall choose, my darling — and all of us happy in a new life. Kim, I know this is a funny time and an even funnier place — but — please, will you marry me?'

'*Marry you* . . . ' The words crept out almost inaudibly as Kim tried to believe what he had just said.

Neil was very close to her. He looked surprised. 'Of course, marry you,' he said urgently. 'Haven't I said that I love you? And you told me you loved me, too — so we get married, don't we, darling?'

Kim tried to hold back her tears, but her joy was so overwhelming that her eyes swam and her voice wobbled as she whispered through a great smile of wonder and sheer happiness. 'Yes, please, Neil. Oh, yes — *please*!'

If stall-holders and visiting villagers watched their embrace, neither Kim nor Neil were aware of it. For a long moment nothing else mattered except the expression of their love and mutual trust in each other.

Then, at last, Neil swung her around, his face almost childish in its uninhibited pleasure. 'Let's go and confront old grumpy Benbow and buy an engagement ring,' he suggested. 'It'll do until we can choose something really special in London.'

Kim's hand was warm in his. 'What a lovely idea. And I don't want something rich and rare from London, thank you. Something made here in Badlake, where we met, is all I want, love.'

In the shadow of Mr Benbow's grudging attention, they chose a beautifully filigreed, yet sturdy, silver ring which shone as a shaft of early spring sunshine slanted into the barn.

'It's perfect. Oh, Neil — thank you.'

He slid it onto her finger, looking deeply into her eyes. 'I'm the one who's truly grateful,' he said quietly, and the listening silversmith edged a few inches nearer, in a vain attempt to understand what was going on right under his nose.

Kim left Neil to pay for the ring and, almost bemused by her sheer happiness, wandered down the tent towards the stall where Jake stood, busily selling models to satisfied customers.

When Neil joined her, she said, 'I wanted Jake to be the first to know, love . . . ' For a second she looked anxiously at his face, but saw only understanding and approval.

'Of course,' he said. And from then on it was easy to draw Jake into the shared warmth of her joy and new-found serenity.

'How have you done, Jake?' Neil asked, before they left the model stall, to go back to Badlake House.

'Better than I'd ever imagined, Mr Leston.' Jake looked shy, yet proud. 'Must have been that reporter. There was a big piece in the local paper about my work today . . . '

'I'm glad.' Kim sighed with relief. It seemed that the rat-faced reporter had actually done something good for once. She pressed close to Neil's side as they walked briskly home, passing the cottage and going on up the drive towards the house, talking happily as they did so.

As Neil closed the front door behind them, and Kim paused in the welcoming hall to remove her anorak and boots, his next words caused a shock of fear to run through her body.

He was looking at her very solemnly, and his voice held that familiar 'no-nonsense' tone. 'Look,' he said carefully, 'I've got a plan. I want us to drive up to London tomorrow. Roger is fine with Mary, and if we leave early, we can be home here by the evening.'

Her heart began to race. 'But — why must we go to London?'

'I want to take you back to the house you lived in with Bruce. Where you killed him. And while we're there

240

you're going to tell me exactly how it happened. Darling, only then will the ghosts be laid for good.'

Dumbly, she stared at him, her thoughts churning in distress. He was right — of course he was. But how was she going to force herself to step back into the haunted past? To actually relive that terrifying, obscene moment when she had killed her husband?

8

Kim sat in the car silent and on edge as Neil drove up the motorway to London early the next morning. Thoughts raced through her mind, always returning to the sad fact that she could no longer escape from reliving the horror of Bruce's death.

In less than two hours they would reach White Gates, the mock Tudor house set in an exclusive London suburb, in which Bruce had invested so much of his prize money.

As the time passed by she realised with a faint sense of gratitude, that Neil, respecting her mood, was making no effort to draw her into conversation. He had spoken only briefly since the journey began, as he slid a classical tape into the cassette recorder under the dashboard.

Gradually the music had penetrated

her fears, its gentle rhythms and harmonies bringing new thoughts with them. Were she and Neil right for each other, coming from such totally different backgrounds?

The music, for instance — she had never gone to classical concerts or operas because Bruce had preferred noisy pop groups. And then there was the huge difference between their styles of living; Neil being very much at home in elegant old Badlake House, while she was more used to the ultra-modern White Gates. Bruce had delighted in commissioning top designers and architects to make their home talked about, and enviable to others.

Again, Kim's nerves began to return. She had been a fool yesterday at the craft show, allowing herself to feel so gloriously happy, for nothing had changed after all.

The sordid fact that, in order to protect her own life, she had killed Bruce must surely ruin whatever future she embarked upon. She would never be free from the feelings of guilt which would plague her for the rest of her days.

Even although Neil was persuading her to tell him the wretched details, with the best will in the world she now feared that he would be so repelled that he would realise their marriage was, after all, quite impossible.

Kim hardly noticed the spring sunshine and the changing landscape as the car travelled smoothly and quickly along. Looking at Neil's handsome, guarded profile beside her, she noticed his eyes were alert with concentration, but there was a sense of relaxation about his mouth and jaw. For a second she felt a stab of envy; if only the music could do as much for her as it obviously did for him.

Then, as the thought flared and died, Neil's hand left the wheel for a second to reach out and touch hers. She watched him smile without taking his eyes off the road, saw his hand return to the wheel, and knew a moment of humility.

Yes, he loved her, and still believed in her. She couldn't let him down, however terrified and reluctant she felt. She loved him too much for that.

If only Bruce had loved her as Neil did.

Kim closed her eyes, lulled by the music and the warmth of the car, and let her mind travel back in time — back to the days leading up to that last frightful night of drama and violence.

* * *

She had been at the ringside when Bruce won the championship medal. Even now, the memory of that tumultuous standing ovation for Britain's new heavy-weight champion made her head reel. God knows, she'd been proud of him, that handsome man who was her husband. If only their young love could have lasted.

Glowing with sweat and pride, Bruce had thrown his arms around her exultantly as he was escorted back to the dressing-room.

'I did it, Kim! At last — at last I'm the champ. Hey, isn't it fantastic? But it's what I planned and worked for all those years. I always knew I'd get it, didn't I? Now we'll really go places, Kim, girl! I said I'd be the greatest, didn't I? Well, I've done it!'

Later they had dined at the showiest, most expensive restaurant in town, Bruce clowning and guffawing as his entourage of fawning supporters continued to praise him to the skies. The wine resulted in some loosened tongues and Kim had felt her old nervousness return when Bruce swayed to his feet and tried to pull her on to the dance floor.

'C'mon, Kim,' he'd mumbled happily, 'let's tread a measure.'

'Not now, Bruce,' she'd pleaded. 'I've got a headache.'

'Headache? You've always got a bloody headache.' The overloud voice reached other ears and Kim heard a wave of quickly muffled laughter sweep through the crowded room.

Bruce's powerful hands yanked her up beside him. 'Tonight you're gonna do what I want. Com'n dance with me — that's an order, or *else*.'

Locked in his arms, her head pulled against his massive shoulder, Kim could smell the alcohol on his breath and knew, wretchedly, that in his hour of triumph Bruce was letting his darker, inner self, come out of hiding. She dreaded what might happen next, for once he was in this outrageous mood no holds were barred.

As if he knew what she was thinking, Bruce bent his head and whispered, in a slurred, thick voice, 'Let's go home, Kim, back to our own li'l pad.'

And then he was pressing her against him, whispering urgently, 'This is my day, Kim, day of a lifetime. Let's make it the night of a lifetime, too, eh? Let's go home, Kim . . .'

She had protested, hoping desperately to keep him there celebrating and drinking with the gang until, as on other occasions, he would pass out, and Joe and his cronies would whistle up a cab and take him home.

She would have done anything to avoid her and Bruce going home to White Gates, where Roger, watched by a baby-sitter, slept peacefully in the quiet night of the exclusive suburb. If they went home now, with Bruce in this amorous and demanding mood, she knew too well what would happen.

But Bruce was adamant. 'I wanna go home! Joe, get me a cab . . . '

Kim heard all Joe's tactful suggestions fall on deaf ears, saw the trainer's unconcealed anxiety and as Bruce led her to the waiting taxi, heard his whispered words in her ear, 'Watch out, Kim, he's a bit beyond himself tonight. Understandable, of course, but still — give me a ring if you need me. Play it cool, give in to him if you must. I mean, he's a big boy to argue with, right? Good luck, love.'

Bruce slept on the way home, his

head heavy on her shoulder, the inside of the taxi reeking with whisky fumes. Kim began to hope that she might slip out unnoticed at the end of the journey and tell the driver to return Bruce to Joe and the others at the restaurant.

However, at the last moment, Bruce opened his eyes blearily, saw Kim getting out, and clumsily heaved himself after her, nearly falling as he stepped on to the pavement.

'Gimme a hand, Kim — that's better . . . '

The taxi driver's voice followed Kim as she staggered beneath Bruce's dead weight. 'Will you be OK, Missus?'

'Yes, thanks.' She longed to scream frantically, 'No, no, I won't! Drive me away from here, for God's sake!' But Roger was asleep in the house and it was unthinkable to leave Bruce alone with his son in this dangerous state.

Jean, the baby-sitter, met them at the door, trying in vain to hide the disgust in her eyes as she said quietly to Kim, 'Roger hasn't stirred, bless him. I'll be off now. Unless — unless I can help in any way?'

Kim had heard that same note of pity in so many other voices. Now she automatically produced a brief, taut smile as she answered, 'No, thanks, Jean. I'll be in touch later in the week. We've — er — been celebrating Bruce's title win. Quite an occasion, you know . . . '

The other woman dropped her eyes. 'Of course. Well — good night, Kim.'

Bruce collapsed in the fashionably-furnished, brilliantly-lit lounge, falling like a log on the huge, white leather couch that stood by the french windows. Kim, standing beside him, wondering what to do next, saw the pale glimmer of moonlight on the swimming-pool out on the terrace and knew she would always remember this moment.

Suddenly her thoughts began to wander. What if Bruce went outside, stumbled, fell into the water? What if he drowned? Bruce dead . . .

She had never envisaged such a thing

before. But now the idea was there, filling her with horror, yet at the same time giving her a nudge of shocking hope. She would be free. She and Roger would at last be able to live a safe happy life.

Then suddenly she realised what she had been thinking, and she was appalled at her own thoughts. Bruce was her husband. In his own, selfish and egotistical way he had been good to her over the years. He had supported her and given her an expensive lifestyle.

It was only the increasing fear of his violence that had undermined their relationship, not a lessening of affection between them, she told herself. But even as all this spun around in Kim's confused mind, the truth suddenly surfaced — she had never really loved Bruce.

When they were young she had been carried away by his good looks and eager charm. Now, shutting her eyes in resignation, she realised too late, that

251

youth was impulsive and unthinking, often bringing unhappiness upon itself by its own actions.

Suddenly, Bruce was awake again, confronting her, swaying and grinning foolishly as he got to his feet. He went across to the bar and poured himself a slopping glass of whisky.

'Wanna drink?' He hiccuped, and she stepped back instinctively.

'No, thanks. And I don't think you ought to have any more.'

No sooner had she uttered the words than she bit her lip, flinching at the obvious look of rage which swept across Bruce's flushed face. 'Don't tell me what to do!' he shouted. 'I'm the champ! I'll do what I want!'

Almost rooted to the spot with fear, Kim watched a sly, little smile spread over his face, replacing his anger, as he added, 'An' what I want right now is you, Kim . . . Come here, girl . . . '

He lurched at her, but she twisted away, watching him stumble; the alcohol had robbed him of the lightness of foot that had helped to make him the legendary fighter he was.

★ ★ ★

Bruce roared her name across the room, the unintelligible sound jarring through her head. Abruptly, her own terror dissolved as she remembered her sleeping son upstairs, and she turned on him.

'Be quiet! Don't make such a row! You'll waken . . . '

It was too late, she snapped the name off. Why, oh why, had she brought Roger into this? Bruce only needed another source of aggravation to make him lose control completely. She was a fool, oh, God what a fool.

'I'll wake my son up if I want to! My son, eh? Namby-pamby li'l brat — I'll make a man out of him, though, see if I don't. Hey, Roger! You hear me up there? Get up, boy! I got things to say to you.'

Now Bruce was trying to climb up

the stairs. It was no easy feat for each step he took he slipped down two. Mumbling and cursing, he pulled himself up by the shining, oak bannister rail, with Kim following, pleading as he did so.

'Bruce, leave him alone, please — *please* — *don't* waken Roger. Look, Bruce, let's go to bed, you're tired, you've had a wonderful day . . . '

'Shut up!'

At the top of the twisting stairs he rounded on her, one enormous hand wildly hitting out and jarring her shoulder, so that she stumbled and nearly fell.

She watched as Bruce staggered off down the passage. He had nearly reached Roger's bedroom door when Kim, clinging weakly to the newel post at the head of the stairs, saw the door open. A small, tousled figure in bright-blue pyjamas appeared, looking scared and vulnerable.

'What is it, Dad?' Roger asked fearfully. 'Mum? Where's Mum? Mum!'

'Here, my darling.' Kim ran down the passage, forcing herself past Bruce as he towered over the frightened child.

'Leave him alone, Kim!' The warning was clear, but she found an unexpected strength and rounded on him.

'No! I'm going to take him away. You're not in a fit state to — '

'I said *leave him alone*!'

Kim kneeled down and put her arms around Roger, who was now weeping noisily against her. She looked up into Bruce's contorted, scowling face, and recognised a danger she'd never seen before. She sensed that this Bruce could actually injure the boy.

All the other past incidents of over-strict punishments, tormenting and mocking the child were nothing to what she now saw in Bruce's obsessed, wild eyes.

She pulled the boy closer to her, fierce in her strength and determination. 'Don't you dare touch him, Bruce. If you try to hurt Roger, I'll — I'll — '

Bruce's hand gripped her hair and

forced her head back to meet his furious gaze. He jeered, 'Yeah? Tell me what you'll do! Go on then — scare me!'

Her answer was clear and unemotional, born of fear and sudden realisation of how much she loved Roger. 'If you as much as touch him, Bruce, I'll kill you. I swear I will.'

Their eyes met with a clashing impact of wills. It was Bruce who, after a few seconds disbelieving silence, turned away and muttered, 'You're crazy!'

Kim, feeling her hair had been pulled out by its roots, bent her head, hardly daring to accept this moment of victory. She kissed Roger's wet cheeks and said, in as quiet and calm a voice as she could manage, 'Darling, we're playing a funny game. Daddy and I will stay here while you see how quickly you can go downstairs and run next door to Jean's house.

'You can reach the bell on her front door, can't you? Go on pressing it till she comes and then say, 'Mummy

256

wants me to stay with you, please, Jean'. Can you remember that, love?'

Her heart pumping, she watched as his fear was replaced by a sudden expression of interest and amusement. 'Can I put my dressing-gown on first?'

'No, darling. In this game you have to be very quick about getting to Jeans' house — you won't have time to feel cold.'

'All right, Mum. Shall I go now?'

'Yes, love.' A lump came into her throat and she pressed him hard against her as the old fear returned. Anything might happen, once Bruce realised Roger was escaping . . . he would probably take it out on her again. It then dawned on her, mistily, that she might never see Roger again . . .

'Go, darling, go quickly. Careful down the stairs. And Roger, be very quiet, love.'

'OK!' He whisked out of her arms and shot off down the passage without another word.

Hardly daring to breathe, Kim

watched as he disappeared down the stairs. She stood tensely, counting the seconds until she heard the front door open and shut again. If only Roger could reach Jean's house before Bruce realised he'd gone . . .

Suddenly, the silence was shattered as Bruce came out of their bedroom, eyes red and glinting, an evil expression on his face. 'I heard the front door open — what are you playing at, Kim?'

Kim weakly got to her feet, thankfully realising that Roger would be out of their garden gate by now, running up to Jean's door and pressing the bell. She walked past Bruce into the bedroom and across to the window. Jean was there, her front door open, taking Roger in. He was safe.

Kim looked round as Bruce entered the bedroom and knew that now Roger had gone, she, too, must leave. It was now or never.

Almost casually, she said, 'I'm not playing at anything, Bruce. I've sent

Roger away. And I'm going as well. I can't stand your drinking and your violence any longer. I'm leaving you, Bruce. And I'm going right now.'

His obvious amazement provided her with some new hope. Perhaps she had taken him so much by surprise that he would actually stand there and watch her go . . . She edged past towards the landing, her eyes holding his, talking as she went.

'Why don't you go to bed? We'll talk about this tomorrow. I'll ring you. You've had such a day, such a wonderful day, you must be tired out. Bruce Hearne, British Champion! Yes, you're the greatest fighter of all time, Bruce. I always knew you'd make it . . .'

The top baluster rail was beneath her fingers. She smiled at him, ready to take that first vital step down towards safety. And then Bruce moved. He was on her before she even saw him coming, his hands snatching roughly at her, pulling her off her feet.

Even as she gasped and let out a scream of absolute terror, he swung her through the open bedroom doorway behind him and dropped her on the big bed.

Winded and scared, she lay there, watching as he slammed the door shut, and then came towards her, face alight with fury and urgency, huge hands tearing at his shirt.

'Leave me? Oh, no! You're mine, Kim. Move over, girl . . .'

★ ★ ★

Kim hadn't realised the Porsche had stopped. Slowly now, she surfaced from her nightmare, to see that they were parked in front of an attractive roadside pub. Neil was looking at her anxiously. 'I thought you were asleep,' he said with concern, 'but I couldn't wake you.'

Kim let out a deep sigh. 'I wasn't asleep,' she replied numbly. 'I was just — remembering.'

Neil's face softened and he touched her cold cheek with a gentle finger. 'Come on in, love, let's have some lunch. We're nearly there, you know. You'll feel better after you've eaten something.'

Kim followed him into a comfortable restaurant close to the cosy bar, and tried to force herself to act normally. But she ate little, and was thankful when Neil glanced at his watch and suggested, 'Let's get on, shall we? The sooner we reach White Gates the sooner this ghastly business will be over, and we can go home.'

Kim noted the unhappy tone of his voice, saw the tension on his unsmiling face, and felt a great wave of love surge through her. He was doing all he could to make her ordeal as quick and easy as possible.

However, the enormity of what lay ahead, suddenly got the better of her churning mind, and, in the privacy of the ladies' cloakroom, she panicked yet again, yielding to the wild urge to run away, to leave Neil and to escape from the trauma that haunted her.

She slipped through a second entrance door into a passageway leading to an exit at the side of the inn. Neil would be waiting in the Porsche — she could leave without him knowing . . .

As she opened the door and felt the fresh spring air on her face she saw him waiting, his expression grim now as he quickly strode towards her. Catching her breath, she felt his hand grasp her wrist and heard the pain and curt disappointment in his words.

'You fool, Kim, I said I loved you — why can't you trust me?'

Vividly remembering Bruce and his fearsome physical domination, Kim was suddenly scared by Neil's strength and determination. She had no stamina left, no more will to fight. Like a cowed animal she allowed him to take her back to the car, and they drove on in a silence broken only by Neil tersely asking for directions to White Gates.

And then the inescapable ordeal

began in grim earnest. Kim saw familiar streets and shops as they reached the suburb she had known so well.

'Turn right by the Post Office, up Woodland Avenue, and left into Thorn Close. White Gates is the last house at the end of the cul-de-sac.'

A 'For Sale' sign stood by the gleaming, wrought-iron gates, and Kim thought the house looked lonely and neglected. The harsh weather had flaked the paintwork, and the garden was a wilderness of overgrown shrubs. She began to tremble as she sat in the parked car, looking at what she had once shared with Bruce.

Neil began to ask questions, turning to her with a reassuring smile, his voice quiet and patient, 'Tell me about Bruce before we go in.'

'I can't. Oh, God, I can't.'

She watched as his smile disappeared and listened numbly as he insisted, 'We've got to go through with this, Kim. It's our only chance of happiness.'

Her nerves jangled. 'Don't bully me, Neil, please.'

'I'm not. I'm simply trying to help you get rid of the ghosts that are threatening to ruin your life. *Our* lives.' He turned to her and smiled, a pleading smile which conveyed more than any words could. 'I know how you feel,' he whispered. 'Please trust me — talk to me.'

At long last Kim was certain that he loved her as much as she loved him. She had to go through with this for both their sakes. She forced herself to think back to that last evening with Bruce and began to tell Neil about the argument at the restaurant, the drive home, the cab driver's concern, and Jean's barely hidden fear. And then about Bruce waking up Roger.

Kim, looking straight ahead of her as she dragged out the story, instinctively hid her face as she told how Bruce had thrown her on to the bed in their room. 'I was so afraid. So terrified . . .'

Neil gently removed her hands from

264

her face. 'It's all right, love, you're safe now. I'm beginning to understand how it all happened. Dear God, what a monster the man was. Look, we must go in. Have you got the key? Be brave for a bit longer, Kim. You've gone through so much, don't break down now.'

Gaining strength from his courage and determination, Kim stifled the threatening tears and nodded her agreement. 'All right. I'm ready.'

Shivering she clung to Neil's hand as they entered the garden and walked up to the large, ostentatious porch, with its mock-Tudor door. Kim's fingers fumbled with the key and Neil took it from her, opening the door and ushering her in.

'We won't waste any time,' he said grimly and led her towards the sweeping staircase. 'You said you were in your room and Bruce had thrown you on to the bed . . . '

They went upstairs in silence, and Kim felt as if the past was shutting

her in. Panic began to build up inside
her and she stumbled, but Neil's arm
was strong around her waist and before
she realised it the staircase was behind
them and they were on the landing.
The landing where, on her knees, she
had whispered so urgently to Roger to
run to safety next door.

Neil's voice interrupted her thoughts.
'Which room?'

Kim couldn't bear to look at him,
instead she simply nodded in the
direction of the master bedroom which
she and Bruce had shared.

'Right. Come on. Let's get it over
with.' Neil's grasp on her hand was
remorseless.

* * *

They entered the room. The long,
pale silk curtains she had once chosen
with such delight, were drawn and
there was a musty smell of perfume
and airlessness. Kim's heart began to
race. She forced herself to look at the

bed. There, on that matching apricot silk cover, she had lain with Bruce threatening her. She felt sick, terrified, disgusted . . .

'Go on. Tell me what happened next,' Neil said.

Kim looked at him, aghast, taking in his stern expression, and the hard line of his compressed lips. Gone was the compassion, the warmth of love, the gentleness which had first drawn her to him.

With a catch in her voice, Kim faltered. 'Don't be angry, don't look at me like that . . . Neil, I can't bear it . . . I thought you loved me?'

He stepped closer, putting his hands on her shoulders, dark eyes large with passion and misery as he said fiercely, 'I do, I do. But don't you see — this is as painful to me as it is to you. You and Bruce, fighting — my parents did the same thing. I've got to put the past behind me as well, Kim. Darling, we're in this together. We've got to go through it together — somehow.'

Finally, Kim understood. His need to relive this last scene was as great and important as hers. By telling him about Bruce and, as a result, exorcising her past, she would help him to forget the pain of his own.

She stood, with Neil's hands still on her shoulders, and discovered that the dreaded words she had thought would be impossible to utter were there, on her lips, waiting to escape.

'Bruce tried to force himself on me. He was drunk and he was furious and rougher than usual. I managed to get away from him — that made him even madder. He . . . ' just once she faltered, but Neil's eyes held hers, giving her the strength to continue. 'I got as far as the kitchen. He caught up with me before I could get the back door open.

'Then he started to throw everything he could lay his hands on. Cups, plates, a kitchen knife . . . ' Abruptly she stopped, seeing the expression in Neil's eyes change.

'It caught me on the cheek and drew blood. I felt it run down my face, sticky and warm. I think that was the final straw . . . ' She gulped, 'I knew then that he was mad, out of control, that if I didn't defend myself he'd probably kill me . . . '

Her uneven words petered out and she began to sob, burying her face in Neil's shoulder. 'I never meant to do it! I just wanted him to stop hurting us — Roger and me — we'd both taken all we could stand. Oh, Neil, Neil, I didn't ever mean it to end like that!'

'Tell me, darling.' Neil's words were almost inaudible.

Kim's hands dropped to her side. She looked deeply into his eyes and sighed. Slowly, she walked away, pausing at the curtained window. Hardly knowing what she did, she pulled one curtain aside.

The silk rustled evocatively and she stared out at the garden path, along which Roger, in his blue pyjamas, had run to safety. The path where later, first Jean, and then two policemen, had walked up to the front door, into the house, and into the kitchen to find her there, staring wildly at Bruce's dead body.

She turned back to look at Neil. 'He shouted that he was going to get me,' she said quietly and without emotion. 'To make me pay for being a rotten wife, for not giving him a daughter, for having a snivelling little coward of a son.

'As he rushed at me I picked up the nearest thing I could find. The knife was there at my feet. I couldn't get away and he was almost on top of me, so I held it in front of me with both hands. He — he stumbled — and fell. On to the knife.'

In the silence of the room her voice came out in a whisper. 'That's — that's how it happened, Neil.'

Time seemed to stop for a moment as she saw once again the look on Bruce's face as he realised what the pain in his chest was. His mouth opening, his eyes full of horror and disbelief. She heard again her own scream filling the room, then felt his body fall on top of her and the blessedness of unconsciousness as at last all was blocked out.

* * *

Now a silence surrounded them as the ghosts from the past slid away and Kim discovered that she was finally able to dismiss the terrible memories. She looked at Neil whose face mirrored her own untold relief.

'Yes, you were right,' she said simply, holding out her hands. 'I've been through it and now it's gone. Oh, please God, it's gone for ever.'

He pulled her into his arms and held her tightly, his kisses warming her and his smile bringing peace to her fraught mind. Kim felt their hearts beating in unison, all the tension and chill of their bodies slowly relaxing in the comfort they gave each other in that long, wonderful embrace.

'Well done, my darling,' he said softly at last, as they parted. 'Come on, let's go home.'

Kim didn't look back as, hand in hand, they left White Gates behind them, got into the car and drove away.

For a few minutes neither of them spoke.

'Music?' Neil asked gently, and Kim shook her head, smiling back at him, her heart overflowing with gratitude and love.

'No music. We've got to talk.'

'We have, indeed. Just think of the misery that might have been avoided if you and Bruce could have really talked.'

Kim touched his hand as it grasped the wheel. 'And if your mother had been able to talk to your father . . .'

'Right.' Thoughtfully, Neil added, 'We'll do better, you and me, love. We'll always talk. About everything.'

Kim nodded. 'Beginning from now. Oh, darling, there's so much I need to tell you, to ask you — to share.'

Neil's eyes held her own for a second and his smile grew. 'So many plans to make. Shall I start, or will you?'

The Porsche seemed to know its own way home. Heading south-west, it purred effortlessly along the motorway towards Devon, Badlake House, and a new future, driving into a spring sunset so vivid that for a moment both Kim and Neil were temporarily blinded.

Neil pulled down the sun-visors and glanced at Kim, as she murmured gratefully, 'Out of the shadows, at last. And into the sunshine . . . '

THE END

PRETTY MAIDS ALL IN A ROW
Rose Meadows

The six beautiful daughters of George III of England dreamt of handsome princes coming to claim them, but the King always found some excuse to reject proposals of marriage. This is the story of what befell the Princesses as they began to seek lovers at their father's court, leaving behind rumours of secret marriages and illegitimate children.

THE GOLDEN GIRL
Paula Lindsay

Sarah had everything — wealth, social background, great beauty and magnetic charm. Her heart was ruled by love and compassion for the less fortunate in life. Yet, when one man's happiness was at stake, she failed him — and herself.

A DREAM OF HER OWN
Barbara Best

A stranger gently kisses Sarah Danbury at her Betrothal Ball. Little does she realise that she is to meet this mysterious man again in very different circumstances.

HOSTAGE OF LOVE
Nara Lake

From the moment pretty Emma Tregear, the only child of a Van Diemen's Land magnate, met Philip Despard, she was desperately in love. Unfortunately, handsome Philip was a convict on parole.

THE ROAD TO BENDOUR
Joyce Eaglestone

Mary Mackenzie had lived a sheltered life on the family farm in Scotland. When she took a job in the city she was soon in a romantic maze from which only she could find the way out.

NEW BEGINNINGS
Ann Jennings

On the plane to his new job in a hospital in Turkey, Felix asked Harriet to put their engagement on hold, as Philippe Krir, the Director of Bodrum hospital, refused to hire 'attached' people. But, without an engagement ring, what possible excuse did Harriet have for holding Philippe at bay?

THE CAPTAIN'S LADY
Rachelle Edwards

1820: When Lianne Vernon becomes governess at Elswick Manor, she finds her young pupil is given to strange imaginings and that her employer, Captain Gideon Lang, is the most enigmatic man she has ever encountered. Soon Lianne begins to fear for her pupil's safety.

THE VAUGHAN PRIDE
Margaret Miles

As the new owner of Southwood Manor, Laura Vaughan discovers that she's even more poverty stricken than before. She also finds that her neighbour, the handsome Marius Kerr, is a little too close for comfort.

HONEY-POT
Mira Stables

Lovely, well-born, well-dowered, Russet Ingram drew all men to her. Yet here she was, a prisoner of the one man immune to her graces — accused of frivolously tampering with his young ward's romance!

DREAM OF LOVE
Helen McCabe

When there is a break-in at the art gallery she runs, Jade can't believe that Corin Bossinney is a trickster, or that she'd fallen for the oldest trick in the book . . .

FOR LOVE OF OLIVER
Diney Delancey

When Oliver Scott buys her family home, Carly retains the stable block from which she runs her riding school. But she soon discovers Oliver is not an easy neighbour to have. Then Carly is presented with a new challenge, one she must face for love of Oliver.

THE SECRET OF MONKS' HOUSE
Rachelle Edwards

Soon after her arrival at Monks' House, Lilith had been told that it was haunted by a monk, and she had laughed. Of greater interest was their neighbour, the mysterious Fabian Delamaye. Was he truly as debauched as rumour told, and what was the truth about his wife's death?

THE SPANISH HOUSE
Nancy John

Lynn couldn't help falling in love with the arrogant Brett Sackville. But Brett refused to believe that she felt nothing for his half-brother, Rafael. Lynn knew that the cruel game Brett made her play to protect Rafael's heart could end only by breaking hers.

PROUD SURGEON
Lynne Collins

Calder Savage, the new Senior Surgical Officer at St. Antony's Hospital, had really lived up to his name, venting a savage irony on anyone who fell foul of him. But when he gave Staff Nurse Honor Portland a lift home, she was surprised to find what an interesting man he was.

A PARTNER FOR PENNY
Pamela Forest

Penny had grown up with Christopher Lloyd and saw in him the older brother she'd never had. She was dismayed when he was arrogantly confident that she should not trust her new business colleague, Gerald Hart. She opposed Chris by setting out to win Gerald as a partner both in love and business.

SURGEON ASHORE
Ann Jennings

Luke Roderick, the new Consultant Surgeon for Accident and Emergency, couldn't understand why Staff Nurse Naomi Selbourne refused to apply for the vacant post of Sister. Naomi wasn't about to tell him that she moonlighted as a waitress in order to support her small nephew, Toby.

A MOONLIGHT MEETING
Peggy Gaddis

Megan seemed to have fallen under handsome Tom Fallon's spell, and she was no longer sure if she would be happy as Larry's wife. It was only in the aftermath of a terrible tragedy that she realized the true meaning of love.

THE STARLIT GARDEN
Patricia Hemstock

When interior designer Tansy Donaghue accepted a commission to restore Beechwood Manor in Devon, she was relieved to leave London and its memories of her broken romance with architect Robert Jarvis. But her dream of a peaceful break was shattered not only by Robert's unexpected visit, but also by the manipulative charms of the manor's owner, James Buchanan.